ECLIPSE
OF THE
HEART

Ronald Tierney

ST. MARTIN'S PRESS
NEW YORK

Design by Junie Lee

Library of Congress Cataloging-in-Publication Data
Tierney, Ronald.
  Eclipse of the heart / Ronald Tierney.
    p. cm.
  "A Thomas Dunne book."
  ISBN 0-312-09792-1
  1. Food writers—California—San Francisco—Fiction.   2. Gay
men—California—San Francisco—Fiction.   3. Puerto Vallarta
(Mexico)—Fiction.   4. San Francisco (Calif.)—Fiction.   I. Title.
PS3570.I3325E28   1993
813'54—dc20   93–24291
                                                                  CIP

First Edition: October 1993

10 9 8 7 6 5 4 3 2 1

For
Goodship
E.D.P.

At night, dogs and coyotes howl. You hear them? The sky is so big. So big, it never stops. And we are lost. All of us. Sometimes we have to feel how lost we are.

—Sali

PROLOGUE

Dear Diary,
I don't want another day like today for at least three years.
At my publisher's request, I attended a special luncheon for the
purpose of tasting this year's new releases from a major Califor-
nia winery. Though my readers probably believe I attend many
such functions, I rarely do.

For forty-five minutes I stood among men in dark suits and
ladies in their elegantly styled-for-daylight gowns, watching
them pluck melon balls drenched in prosciutto butter off little
silver trays in a restaurant which resembles a whorehouse far
more than the internationally famous restaurant it is.

I'm sorry. I've never really been in a whorehouse and I'm re-
ally not quite sure I could imagine it; but the red-flocked wall-
paper and gaudy, dripping chandalier crystals had the feel of
old, bawdy San Francisco—you know, pirates and prostitutes
from whose stock all the city's current reigning families de-
scend.

I was just becoming comfortable, gauging wrongly it turns

out, that my anonymity was secure, that I could dine and go, when I heard the mâitre d' mention my name to a small cluster of Epicureans. Being anything but sociable, I managed to brush away the immediate swarm of attention by suggesting that it must be time to eat and rushing headlong to my table.

The service was slightly pretentious, but prompt. I coasted through the first dish, a single ravioli stuffed with braised shrimp, floating in pea-green cream. I was able to nod, shake my head, and smile at the questions of my tablemates until, discouraged rather than insulted, they turned to each other for conversation.

I sipped a new wine with each new course. We were nearing the end. The waiters brought out the entree. The menu spoke:

BABY QUAIL, STUFFED WITH FOIE GRAS, NESTED ON A BED OF JU-LIENNE OF SNOW PEAS, MADEIRA SAUCE, GARNISHED WITH NASTUR-TIUM FLOWERS.

Unfortunately, I hadn't taken the nest idea quite so literally. There was, indeed, a nest—an incredibly realistic nest, constructed from finely slivered snow peas, woven with great care. Inside the nest were two tiny birds, the naked babies of mother quail, prostrate, their miniscule, featherless arms raised above them in a gesture of absolute horror.

Zachary, San Francisco, July

2

1 He'd only intended to glance in quickly. After all, it was night. There were lights on inside. But he'd been caught. And now it was awkward. The last thing in the world he enjoyed was having to make conversation with strangers.

"You're Zachary Grayson, aren't you?" she said, unlocking the glass door to the gallery.

"I'm sorry. I didn't mean to bother you. Looks like you have work to do."

"No," the attractive, fortyish woman said. "You must come in. We're putting up the new show. Come in, I insist."

Zachary never knew what to do when people insisted. He went into the bright lights, stepped through remnants of large, wooden crates. His eyes caught on a huge, colorful canvas and discovered—much to his discomfort—that it was a male nude.

"Such wonderful things are coming out of Spain these days," she said, moving next to him at the very moment he wished to move on. "The artists in Spain and Barcelona are so uninhibited, don't you think?

"Seems so," he said. He looked around for a more comfortable place to rest his eyes.

"My name is Alva Burdine. I'm in the process of closing down my gallery in Washington, D.C., and relocating here permanently and completely."

"It's a very nice gallery, Ms. Burdine."

"Alva. I have all your books. I've lined them up on the shelf above the refrigerator." She swept back a swirl of hair that had escaped the ponytail she no doubt wore only while doing manual labor. She smiled. "I have to confess I'm quite capable of screwing up a three-minute egg, but it impresses the hell out of everyone who wanders into the kitchen."

He liked her. He still wished to escape and was about to excuse himself with some vague hint at a deadline when a dark-haired young man, also with a ponytail, approached them.

"This is Henry. Henry, this is Zachary Grayson."

Henry, who hadn't seemed to have noticed the intruder, looked up at him suddenly and extended his hand.

"The writer. What a pleasure."

Henry's hand was warm, his handshake intimate, held a few seconds too long.

Zachary walked to California Street to catch the cable car. He had no intention of trying to scale the hills on his own weary legs. On the way he'd had an ugly and frightening encounter with one of the street crazies—a man who called him a "bourgeois pouf" and threatened to take Zachary's tie and strangle him with it.

The man did no harm. One sudden lurch in Zachary's direction seemed to have satisfied his hostile urges and the man moved on.

Once at home, in bed under the goose-down comforter, a book open on his lap, and a glass of sherry on the bedside table, Zachary managed to find the evening as amusing as it was unsettling. It had been a long time since anyone had flirted with him. Certainly no one as young and good-looking as Henry. And he believed he had been fortunate to have been threatened by someone literate and creative enough to formulate the expression "bourgeois pouf" instead of the usual stream of predictable obscenities.

Fortunately, he thought, he would see none of them again. He would be more careful in the future. The last thing he wanted was an eventful day.

Some hours later, Zachary awoke, cold. He could feel the sweat on his face. He couldn't remember it. He didn't want to remember it. He was sure it was the dream. Perhaps the events of the day. Perhaps the sushi. But it was the dream.

The square opening was a window, but it held no glass. It was merely a frame for the changing Mexican sky. Nor was there a door in the doorway. It, too, let in the heavy night air, the sound of the waves, and, in between their lapping, the gentle trickle of the creek that passed by the small concrete structure.

"Sali?" asked the familiar voice.

Sali, lying flat and still upon his mat, had felt the presence before the voice. He had heard the breathing. He had been prepared to fight or run. Now, relieved, he started to pull the thin blanket over his nakedness, forgetting for a moment that it made no difference. The old man was blind.

5

"Bat?" Sali asked, the goose pimples on his flesh subsiding.

"I hope I haven't frightened you too much," the old man said, "but remember I said one day I might ask you to do me a favor?"

In the D.C. suburb of Georgetown, Jeremiah Tower sat at the desk in his study. He'd just completed one call and was punching in another number. He let it ring twice, disconnected, and punched the redial button. As it rang, he tapped his well-manicured fingernails against the green-and-black marble. The harsh light of the desk lamp revealed the light brown liver spots on the back of his hand. He stopped tapping and dropped the hand into the pocket of his robe.

"It's moving," Tower said into the phone.

"Where?" the voice asked.

"Somewhere in Mexico."

"Why didn't they call me?"

"That's a good question, isn't it, Jessup?"

"Yes, sir. Don't worry. We'll get it."

"Damned right you will," Tower said and hung up.

They always knew where to find him. This time it was a seedy resort in Key West. The ugly voice on the other end of the phone asked if he was alone.

"I don't know yet," Manny said. "I think so." He felt fingers running along the nape of his neck and down his back. "I guess not."

"For Christ's sake, then, just listen. There's a hotel in Fort Lauderdale. The Dobriani Beach. Atlantic Boulevard. Know it? If you do, just grunt."

Manny grunted.

"Get your young ass over there. Check in before nine this morning," the voice said.

"How come you get up so early?"

"Nine. Not nine-fifteen. Got it?"

"What name?"

"No time. Use the one you're using now."

Click.

Manny didn't know the guy he was talking to. Just the ugly voice. It was the anonymous voice of his employer, or more likely, the anonymous voice of one of his employer's minions. Chances were there were dozens of shadows between the voice and the top boogieman. He didn't like his employer, whoever the hell it was, and he was pretty sure he or they didn't like him. All he got was shit work.

It all started innocently enough. They needed a guy from the company who spoke Spanish—Cuban Spanish. They needed him in a hurry. That was four years ago, when Manny at twenty-eight was little more than a raw recruit with a heavy linguistics background.

When the emergency was over, the company didn't take him back. So he was permanently dumped in this secret organization inside a secret organization. He thought of it as one of the box gigs, where each box you open has another box inside. Manny was in the smallest box.

Now, at thirty-two, it was clear Manny wasn't exactly on a skyrocketing career path. He was little more than a courier, a messenger boy, who with the help of brown contacts to cover his green eyes, could pass as Cuban, Mexican, or Chilean for that matter. And often did.

"What's up?" said the pretty voice that belonged to the warm body pressing up against his back.

"I gotta go," Manny said. He rolled over to face her.

7

"Where? The bathroom or somewhere else?"

"Somewhere else. You got the room for five more days."

"That's it, huh? Bye, nice knowing you?"

"Yeah. I mean we did all right. Had a good time. We didn't just screw. We talked, didn't we?"

"Right," she said. "You got a wife, three kids, and this was just one more alcoholic, sex-filled binge in the tropics."

"True."

"No, it's not true," she said, putting her hand on his thigh. "That's not your story, at least not the part about the wife and kids."

"Okay," he said.

"Whatever I say, right?" she said. "It doesn't make any difference."

She was pretty, with short ash blond hair and small, firm breasts.

"Sure. That's the best part. I can be anybody you want. A girl with imagination can fill in the blanks."

"Yeah, well, I don't have much of an imagination. I'm a realist," she said, her hand moving up between his legs.

"I don't know your story either, do I? So I get to make up one. You're a famous European actress getting away from it all."

"I don't even have an accent," she said, laughing.

"Yes you do. Wisconsin. Near Milwaukee."

"Shit."

"True or false?" He got out of bed. She watched him walk naked to the bathroom. He was a little wobbly. He looked in the mirror.

"On the nose," she said.

He could barely hold onto the toothbrush. "Steady boy," Manny said to the mirror. He'd seen the sun come up a thousand times, but he didn't like to wake up to it.

2 Zachary always got up before it was light. He stumbled into the kitchen and ground a fraction of an inch of vanilla bean, adding it to his filtered morning coffee. Then, leaning against the counter, he drank a large glass of grapefruit juice, convinced it would melt away the small roll of flesh that had gathered at his near middle-aged waist. Zachary was keenly aware he was only two years shy of the half-century mark.

When the coffee was ready, he took the large mug with him to the desk in the bedroom and sat as the sun rose over San Francisco Bay. He rolled one of the ten cigarettes he would smoke during the day—two with coffee—and watched the dark form of Alcatraz take shape in the fog. It was always an ominous sight—an every-morning birth of the ugliest chunk of rock in the world—when the fog didn't obliterate it entirely.

Sometimes he wondered if it might not change his life to have maybe a palm tree instead of a prison to start his day.

Zachary pulled out his journal, picked up his Mont Blanc

fountain pen, and dipped into the deep black Pelikan ink bottle to fill it for the day's writing. He took great pleasure in ritual and an even greater pleasure in beauty. Expensive pens, like expensive coffee and tobacco, meant little as status symbols. They couldn't. There were few people who would ever see them. He didn't get out much, not really. However, beauty and quality gave Zachary a sense of peace and comfort that far outweighed the cost of owning them.

Zachary pulled out his journal and began to write what he referred to as his "personal drivel." The second ritual—this combination of coffee, cigarettes, and drivel—helped him become coherent, he believed, and was absolutely essential for more productive work as the morning wore on.

Like a turtle's pond, Zachary's San Francisco condominium, on the corner of Green and Greenwich, had been his hiding place for twenty years, from which he emerged for essentials and a few social functions demanded by his profession.

From his bedroom window, he could see the steep descent of Green Street to the bay. Out of his living room window was Telegraph Hill, topped by Coit Tower, an illuminated, ostentatious phallus, built by some deceased matron to honor San Francisco's firemen. There were stories about how she came to choose that particular design.

Aside from the bedroom he slept in, Zachary had two others, one he used as an office and library, and the third kept freshly sheeted and clean for guests, though no one had ever spent a night in it.

The kitchen looked to nothing. It was a cave. Besides the glass-doored refrigerator and a restaurant-styled iron stove, the room was cluttered with copper and iron cookware, large wooden spoons, metal ladles, two food processors, two additional, small ovens—one convection, the other a microwave. Iron skillets. Open shelves with every spice known to man, several coffee canisters. A library of cookbooks. Dozens of glass jars, labeled in his own hand, containing fresh herbs and spices.

Typically, after penning a few notes in his journal, Zachary would spend two hours on real writing, the writing that enabled him to keep himself in the comfort to which he'd grown accustomed. Today he would attempt to finish the third chapter of his book on Amerasian cuisine. Then he would go to Chinatown about noon and visit Huy Sen's food market. Afterward, he would come home and work in his small garden.

His plans, however, were disturbed by the unpleasant ringing of his telephone.

If Zachary talked to anyone regularly, besides his editor in New York, it was his neighbor Leslie. And he wouldn't talk to Leslie, if Leslie weren't the persistent type.

"So I take it young Henry is quite smitten with you, dear boy," Leslie said when Zachary, who took morning interuptions of his work unkindly, answered the phone.

"What?"

"Alva Burdine."

Zachary had already misplaced the name. It sounded familiar but was lost in the gray matter of a brain focusing the varying qualities of California and French olive oil.

"What are you talking about?"

"Alva Burdine. Gallery. Last night. Boy meets legendary guru of exotic cuisine. Boy falls madly in infatuation. What does object of affection have to say about all of this?"

"Legendary guru says good-bye to legendary gossip."

Zachary was always surprised at how small a town San Francisco was.

* * *

Five minutes past ten, the ugly voice on the phone gave Manny the name of a bar in Miami.

"You're an hour late," Manny said.

"Sue me."

"You send me up here to Fort Lauderdale to a hotel where guys with dagger tattoos are passed out by the pool from a crack-filled high the night before and now you tell me I'm supposed to go to Miami? Why didn't you tell me to go to Miami in the first place?"

Manny wanted a shot of tequila more than he wanted a million dollars.

"There's a guy there. Cuban. Has something for you to do."

"Do I wait until somebody sings 'Babaloo' or does this Cuban have a name?"

"He's got twenty or thirty of them. Big guy. Can't miss him."

"When?"

"Now."

It wasn't far. Just off the 79th Street Causeway. The bar was a night club of sorts; but it was eleven in the morning, and while the place was open it didn't look it. Nobody in the place except for a bartender—who wore a white shirt and black bow tie—sipping coffee, and a 350-pound Cuban sitting with some guy who Manny thought was altogether too hairy to look good in a tank top.

Manny went to the bar first, ordered a margarita "up." He took a couple of sips and looked around.

"Somebody spent a fortune to make this place look cheap," he said to the bartender.

"You a decorator?" the bartender asked, grinning, "or just a sensitive guy?"

"A sensitive guy."

"Hey, in a couple minutes the place is all tits and ass. Nobody gives a shit about the wallpaper."

"That the owner?" Manny asked, nodding toward the big Cuban.

"He says he is."

"That's good enough for me," Manny said.

"A bit of advice—don't go knocking the decor of this place. He's a sensitive guy, too."

The table was near the dance floor. Little diamonds of light from the mirrored ball flashed across the big Cuban's white shirt and silver hair. The T&A lunch crowd was coming in all at once.

"Talk to me," Manny said in Spanish.

The Cuban looked up, then over at his table companion. The hairy guy got up abruptly, retreating to a dimmer recess of the club. The Cuban smiled. The music got louder. Manny knew he wasn't going to like what the man had to say.

Zachary loved San Francisco. He'd come there from the Midwest when he was twenty-three, when the whole Bay Area had moved from birthing the great bohemian movement to the years of the flower children. The city had gone through some rough times. The hippies had crashed and burned. Haight-Ashbury, once alive with new thought and new hope, had filled with desolation. Afterward, the neighborhood tried to get itself back together, but it still suffered an identity crisis— young professionals, stubborn, recalcitrant hippies, and gays struggled to own it.

Then AIDS crept into the city, slowly at first, but soon it became an occupying force. The devastation of AIDS and the subsequent loss of many of the people who gave the city its vital, creative personality, put the most politically progressive municipality in the nation into a long, debilitating period of mourning. The spirit seemed more than dampened, it had been suffocated. Just as it was learning to cope and conquer, the earthquake hit. The almost cavalier nature that natives once had about earthquakes turned to an increased and jittery awareness of mortality.

But, as they always had, the inhabitants were willing to fight any oppressor, including disease, depression and self-pity. They were willing to resurrect hope. It didn't surprise Zachary. Hope, endurance, and the willingness to accept sacrifice are the qualities of an immigrant population. And the immigrants, whether they were from the Middle East or the Midwest, whether they were settled for generations or recently arrived from some strange land, kept the city alive and vital. They did so despite the obstacles, despite, or perhaps because of, the difference the various cultures brought to the city.

It was that part that Zachary loved. What he liked best were the neighborhoods, where as a resident tourist walking a few short blocks, he could feel the cultures of the world—all here, in one incredibly inhabitable city. Of the neighborhoods, he tended to favor Chinatown. He preferred Stockton Street over the touristy Powell. On Stockton, you could walk the length of it and never see a white face or hear a white language. The people, the store signs, the newspapers, the clothing, the smells were all Chinese. It could be Hong Kong or Shanghai in the old days.

Huy Sen would talk to Zachary in broken English as he guided the American author through his store. They held each other in mutual esteem, Huy Sen showing him the latest import or the freshest fruits and vegetables. Not just a nice, gentle man, Huy Sen was also a shrewd businessman and he good-naturedly but constantly lobbied for mention in one of Zachary's books.

"Today I show you some very good rice," Huy Sen told Zachary.

"I don't need rice today, Huy Sen, I am looking for . . ."

"Ah, Mr. Grayson—who does not need rice?

"I don't. I have several huge burlap bags from earlier trips to your store. One man can eat only so much."

"This is new to America. First time." Huy Sen led Zachary through the rows of wooden platforms that held a myriad of fruits and vegetables. "Maybe your new book can mention Mr. Huy Sen and his new rice. Maybe?"

Yellowish light came through a small window at the top of one of the walls in the small room behind the store. Zachary could barely see. When they finally adjusted to the darkness, Huy Sen's hands were already sifting handfuls of long-grained rice from a wooden barrel.

"If I could mention names, the name of Huy Sen would be in all of my books," Zachary said. "You've been very kind to me. But if I mention your name, then every grocer, cookware producer, and catsup maker in the world will be at my door."

Huy Sen looked up, smiled. "I know that, Mr. Grayson. Maybe I can bribe you." Huy Sen winked.

Zachary smiled. "I don't need the money, Mr. Sen."

"Who talks money, Mr. Grayson? I have something much better for you."

Huy Sen went to the door and closed it, bringing down a wooden two by four to secure it.

"You're going to hold me for ransom?" Zachary said, kiddingly.

"No. Much better." He went to the dilapidated wall shelving that held dusty, sealed jars of liquid. Zachary couldn't even guess at the contents.

"Some magical ingredients? Love potions?"

"You want love potion, Mr. Grayson?" Huy Sen smiled.

"My goodness, I'd hardly know what to do with it."

"No. Much better." Huy Sen pulled out two metal pins, then tugged at the shelving. Behind it was a door into darkness.

3 So what it was was this: Manny would go to San Francisco. He would befriend some gay guy who wrote cookbooks for a living. Then he would wait for further instructions. Why, he didn't know. Was this Zachary character giving highly classified recipes to the North Koreans?

The 350-pound Cuban smiled, but Manny was sure he wasn't smiling at the joke. What he was smiling about was Manny and "the faggot."

"You are instructed to get close to him," the Cuban said. Big grin. "Very close." He laughed. His body laughed, fat rolling from his neck to his waist. He handed Manny an eight-by-ten envelope, struggled to get up, then left Manny standing.

"Did anybody ever tell you you bear a striking resemblance to Fred Astaire?" Manny said to him.

The Cuban turned, stopped, turned back toward Manny, but he wasn't smiling. He said something.

A blonde, a well-built woman-child with a ponytail, was on stage. That was all Manny could see. All Manny could hear was the word "dangerous" and that was in the song—"dangerous" riding over the heavy bass.

"My best to the wife and kids, okay?" Manny said and left.

Manny took a taxi to the airport. "Goodbye warm weather, hello fog," he said as the plane picked up speed. Through the little window, he saw the palm trees begin to blur a bit.

He really didn't mind the change. Key West seemed to encourage an already bad alcohol habit. There wasn't anything to do there but drink and look at the funny tourists. If he could remember her last name or the address, perhaps he could track down Sarah in San Francisco. No, it wasn't Sarah. The name began with an *s*. Sally? No. Suzie. That was it. Suzie. Suzie with a *z*—a really funny, sexy, dark-haired girl who didn't mind or didn't care where Manny came from or where he was going.

Now could he remember Suzie's last name? Her phone number? He didn't even remember what name *he* was using at the time. But he remembered it was on Stanyan and if she hadn't moved, he could have a good time.

Manny felt the plane lift. He closed his eyes. Takeoffs always put him to sleep. He'd wake up when he heard ice falling into little plastic glasses.

Zachary was impressed. There *was* an underground. The long tunnels were still there, stone steps leading up from the dank passageways to shops that opened onto the streets.

Unfortunately, the wonderful visions that had always filled Zachary's mind—ancient men with small beards and straw hats sitting, smoking pipes that emitted a purple opium haze—failed to materialize. Nor were there crowds of gamblers babbling in Mandarin as he'd read about and imagined.

"Is there a way out of here?"

"No. Walls built. Close off. Many other places, Mr. Grayson. I can tell stories."

After leaving Huy Sen's, Zachary stopped a few blocks away at City Lights Bookstore in North Beach, and picked up two books. Then, very much according to ritual, he went next door to Vesuvio's for an Anchor Steam. He had the feeling from the spicket that he'd just stepped back twenty or thirty years. The clocks at both places were on western bohemian time, stuck in an era in which Zachary felt comfortable.

Zachary sat by the window and opened one of the books, Sam Shepherd's *Motel Chronicles,* but his mind was still on the underground tunnels Huy Sen had shown him and he filled his brain with long-stemmed opium pipes and a clatter of quibbling voices in the dim light of kerosene lanterns.

It wasn't a fair exchange, really. Zachary had promised to mention Huy Sen in the book he was writing—and he'd do it somehow—but Huy Sen had made him promise not to talk about the secret passageways for twenty years.

The wise old man with the ponytail had outsmarted the foolish, famous author. In twenty years, Huy Sen would be dead and there was a reasonable chance Zachary would be too.

Back home, Zachary changed into his Bermuda shorts and T-shirt and went out to his garden. He couldn't grow much. The plot of ground was too small and most of it was in the shade. Because San Francisco wasn't known for its sunny disposition, Zachary grew herbs that could take a frequent chill and a dim sun.

There was a small patch of daylilies. There was also foxglove. This was his favorite. Aesthetically, foxglove conjured up old-style gardens. Practically, one could conjure from it a substance known as digitalis. One day, hovered over an old book, Zachary himself had morbidly created the deadly substance which he eventually put into a small pink packet and tucked in his wallet.

There were two reasons he coveted the small pack of instant death. One was merely a perverse pleasure in possessing the evidence of nature's basic ambivalence. Nature, he believed, is neither inherently kind nor inherently unkind, good nor evil. It simply was. The acceptance of that fact kept him free from regretting the past and expecting too much of the future. The second and more important reason he kept the means of ending life so close to him was a practical consideration.

There was no one he wished to murder. He knew no one well enough to love, let alone hate. The only person he was even remotely close to was Leslie from across the hall, whom Zachary considered more of an entertainment than a friend. Though Zachary had no death wish, he wanted a quick and painless option to life, should it be necessary.

This seed of a suicidal notion had nothing to do with his being homosexual or growing old or being alone, though all of those things were true. He had come to terms with all three. What it had to do with was something he understood to be an irrational fear—not the usual fears of enclosed places, or heights, or water, but of simply forgetting.

That strange fear of forgetting had been reinforced by a recurring dream that had him sitting on a white stone bench in the middle of an unfamiliar plaza. The sun would be shining. There would be harsh shadows. The buildings would be bleached white. There would be countless arches, entryways, and stairways. There would be no noise, no people. And Zachary would know nothing. He wouldn't know why he was there, what he was supposed to do or where he was supposed to go.

The only signs of life in this private piece of film crackling on the screen of his unconsciousness would be crows, two or three black birds that stood watching him in a way that the dreamer interpreted as expectation. Of what, he had no idea.

For Zachary, crows signified a mark of transition in real life. He saw them when he was six, as he walked his mother to the automobile one summer afternoon. She never returned. He heard their calls the night his father died ten years later. There were other times as well. And in each case, it marked a significant end to something or someone.

When Zachary was far removed from the occurrence of the dreams he often thought about them. The images would simply pop into his mind without the least provocation and certainly without invitation. He couldn't imagine why the dream and the half-life of its cinematic rerun terrified him so much. But it did. Forgetting was, or should be, a painless surgery.

He had, in fact, already forgotten much of his own past, or at least filed it so far away it was no longer real. His father had forgotten so much before he died. So had his father's mother. Did Zachary possess the gene of forgetfulness? Would he forget where he lived, what he did for a living? Perhaps he would forget how to speak, how to understand what simple words meant. If he ever got to such a state there would be, of course, no point to anything. He would kill himself—provided of course he could remember he had the little packet of poison in his wallet and what he was supposed to do with it.

Today the thought passed through his mind quickly. He was content. For him, the day had been rich. He had finished the third chapter of his new book and he had seen part of the secret passageways of Chinatown. What more could you ask for in one day of a life?

* * *

"Forty-eight years on one fucking page," Manny said out loud. "Not much of a life, is it?" He threw the thin folder containing the report and a Xerox copy of a black-and-white photograph of Zachary Grayson on the well-worn bedspread.

Manny moved to the window. They had put him up in some dump of a hotel in San Francisco's Tenderloin district. Below, by nine at night, there was already business on the streets: Sex, drugs, but not a lot of rock and roll.

It was a part of the city where many of its inhabitants weren't hanging on day-by-day. They hung hour-by-hour. Below, the street people would shout and curse, try to get a warm body for the night or score their drug of choice to alter their reality. With a little luck, they wouldn't have to face it again until morning.

Why did Manny's assignments always end up seedy and sordid? Good question, he thought. Why was his life so seedy and sordid, a step away from the street life below whether he was on assignment or not? That was a better question. Surely there were assignments to be had among the rich and famous. Maybe this Zachary character was a ticket off the freighter and onto a luxury liner.

From the dossier, Manny knew where Zachary Grayson lived. He knew that the man's address on Green Street was a helluva lot better than this one. Manny knew the guy wrote a food column. A couple of bestsellers. Worth a small fortune, probably. Manny also knew the guy led the life of an eighty-year-old widow. A safe, scheduled life. Unrelentingly uneventful. A life even a third-grader could accurately abbreviate for the company. This Zachary character was rich, famous and yet for Manny this would be about as exciting as checking into an accountants' convention.

One page and Manny knew where Grayson bought his

shirts, his groceries, stationery, and toilet paper. He knew Grayson liked movies, frequented a Japanese hair stylist, that he favored a bakery on Union Street and wandered for hours in a variety of bookstores. He dined out regularly. Alone.

Zachary Grayson. Born: Kansas City, 1944. Education: University of Missouri, Journalism. Probably homosexual according to interviews with former classmates. No current sexual activity. However, he can be found Friday nights at the Elite Café on Fillmore Street. Before they closed, Grayson used to have drinks at J.J.'s Piano Bar and the Alta Plaza, both on Fillmore and both known homosexual establishments.

There were a few regular haunts, apparently. On Thursdays, he had lunch at the Patio Café on Castro Street. Then he would spend an hour or two at a bookstore down the street known to specialize in homosexual literature.

Zachary Grayson's predictable life made Bernard Manning's life easier. Tomorrow was Thursday. The two of them would meet at the Patio Café.

Zachary Grayson went to a movie at the Lumiere on California Street later in the afternoon, went home, and had a couple of slices of cheese, an apple and a glass of wine.

He tried reading Italo Calvino's *Difficult Loves*, but found it too difficult and instead read several chapters of a Margaret Atwood mystery—an English and therefore more comfortable book. At nine, he took a bath, slipped on a pair of ivory silk pajamas and climbed into bed.

With the electronic remote, he clicked on the VCR, and picked up Luchino Visconti's film of the book, *Death in Venice,* at the spot where he'd left it last night. He remembered Leslie's argument that it was Thomas Mann's "gay book."

Zachary had agreed that it had a homoerotic nature, but

23

that "it was about beauty and death more than sexual orientation."

"Nothing is ever sexual with you, Zachary," Leslie had said.

It was true enough. Zachary clicked off the light and wondered if he'd stay awake to the end.

"Suzie," Manny said when she opened the door to her Stanyan Street home.

"Brad," she said smiling, though apparently not surprised.

"Yes," Manny said, suddenly not only recognizing the name he'd given her then, but recognizing instantly what it was he liked about her. "Surprise."

"I suppose it is," she continued to smile; but Manny, a.k.a. Bradley Davis, knew that her mind was buzzing at Mach II. "Come on upstairs. There's someone I want you to meet."

He followed her up the long, steep stairway into her second-floor railroad flat. Whoever it was up there—a mother, a kid, her new old man—he definitely didn't want to meet and had he not been absolutely mesmerized by her dark eyes and sensuous lips, and her memorable butt, now at eye level, he would have begged off.

"You're a lucky guy," he found himself telling the blond-haired kid she introduced as her fiancé. The smile that went with it hurt.

At ten the following morning—and still suffering from a post-Suzie-and-her-beau trauma and a subsequent hour-long tequila binge—Manny made his way to San Francisco's shopping mall on Market Street. He went up the spiral escalators until he reached the Barnes & Noble bookstore. He found Zachary Grayson's book, *Pacific Nouvelle Cuisine*. The pic-

24

ture on the back was a lot clearer than the darkened Xerox likeness in the dossier. The author had a kind, passive face.

Manny flipped through the book. He'd never be able pick up enough to talk cooking with Grayson, whom he planned to meet in a few hours. He moved through the aisles and found a book on Passolini. An autobiography. Maybe he could talk film with Grayson. They had that in common. He read a chapter standing there, then bought the book and went up to the little café in Nordstrom's and with coffee and a croissant, continued to read until noon.

He took one last look at the dossier before he flushed it down the john. He descended the escalators until he got to street level, deciding he still had time to walk to Castro Street. As he joined the sea of people on Market Street, Manny wondered how his own dossier would read.

Carlton Bernard Manning. He hated "Carlton" and wasn't too fond of "Bernard." Born: Jersey City, New Jersey. Parents: Retired in Phoenix suburbs, now dead, probably from boredom, leaving the entirety of their estate to a cat-care center. Siblings: None. Education: Columbia University. Current Employment: Classified. So classified even he didn't know.

Current associates: None. Sexual proclivities: Yes. After alcohol, the second most important thing in his life. Definitely heterosexual, but wondered what he'd do if there were no women around. Armed and dangerous? Sometimes. Weaknesses: Alcohol and sex. Eating habits: Peanuts at the bar or Burger King. Favorite dance: Last Tango in Paris.

What else? Some girl, a hairstylist in Houston, told Manny that he was a Libra and that in the Chinese zodiac he was a rabbit. Sounded right to him. A lot of fucking and hopping around. Maybe a dangerous rabbit like the one that attacked

Jimmy Carter. What else? Oh yeah, the girl also said he had a nice ass.

Suzie told him that too, years ago. Ah, Suzie. The last and best thing was what Suzie told him when she showed him out last night: "I'm not a nun," she said. And her kiss wasn't sisterly. He was glad he'd glanced at Suzie's phone and memorized her phone number.

4 The first phase of Manny's mission—getting close to Zachary Grayson—was accomplished easily. There was the phony chance encounter at the Patio Café on Castro. Manny, who waited outside until he saw Grayson go in, found a seat next to the famous author and opened the book on Passolini. A conversation on the merits of the rebel filmmaker was struck even before the waiter arrived.

"What do you recommend?" Manny asked.

Zachary looked up. "The chicken salad is nice."

"Thanks, that's what I'll have. My name is Bernard Manning." He hated to use his real name but the out-of-the-blue assignment gave him no time to prepare a convincing false identity.

"Mine is Zachary . . . uh . . . Grayson."

"The famous culinary expert. I guess I know who to ask for a menu suggestion, don't I?"

"I hope so. For both our sakes. You read cookbooks, do you?" he asked glancing over to the book on Manny's table.

"No. I usually dine on canned vegetable soup and Hostess cupcakes. But I've heard the name. Craig Claiborne, James Beard, Zachary Grayson."

"You've put me with the old guard. I don't know whether to be upset or flattered. I'll try flattered for a while. You're a Passolini fan?"

"The book? Well, not really. I've only seen *Canterbury Tales* and *Arabian Nights*. Visually pretty striking, but . . ." Manny shrugged. He wondered if he was convincing. He hadn't seen any Passolini films. His taste was more toward *9½ Weeks*.

"You're a rare one," Zachary said. "Most people—critics, I mean—find themselves either devoted fans or passionate foes."

"Ah critics, what do they know?"

Zachary laughed. "We know surprisingly little."

On Friday, the second "accidental meeting" found Manny and Grayson chatting at the Elite Café bar.

Manny's connection with Grayson was so easy, it was scary. The gaffe at their first meeting—Manny telling the food critic that critics didn't know much—had helped more than hindered what appeared to be a now budding friendship. During the two hours the two sat there, they talked and Manny "just happened to mention" that his apartment had gone condo, that he'd waited too long to find a place, and that now he was struggling to find one. He was rapidly running out of money staying at hotels, he told Grayson. Grayson almost bit.

What did transpire from the conversation was an agreement to meet for dinner the next night, Saturday, at a Thai restaurant south of Market, across the street from Hamburger Mary's.

The place was crowded, the food was excellent. Zachary, used to dining alone and drinking modestly, was seduced by the company and encouraged by the spicy food to drink more than usual.

Before the check came, Zachary had so lost his inhibitions, he had actually invited the young stranger to stay with him. Then insisted.

He had three bedrooms, Grayson said, one used to sleep, one he used for his office, and one available for guests. Why didn't Manny stay there for a while until he found a place? After a few polite objections, Manny became Zachary's room-mate.

Though Manny could have moved in that evening or certainly the following morning, Manny wanted to make another connection before he gave up his lurid private life.

He did. Manny connected with Suzie what's-her-name. And it too was easy. He called Suzie. She was up for it. He gave her his room number.

"Comin' down in the world, Brad," Suzie said, coming into the hotel room. "You rent this by the hour?" She bounced on the bed. "What is this, Leona Helmsley's convict theme room?" She smiled and slipped off her gray sweatshirt.

Her breasts were just as he had cataloged them in his personal encyclopedia of lust. She smiled, her dark eyes looking up at him. "C'mon," she said, tugging playfully at his zipper, "it's my bacherlorette party. So what if there's no cake."

Yes, yes, yes, he remembered her.

Afterward, they lay together on the dingy gray sheets. Ghostly daylight seeped in from one small, smoke-yellowed window that faced a brick wall.

"I kinda liked doing it here," she said, lifting her head and looking into his eyes, "in this place with those ugly draperies and the burn holes in the blanket."

"Just the right touch of tawdry to set off the sleaze. I know what you mean. I was hoping the decorator could do my place when I get one."

"I should have worn maybe a black garter belt and brought along a couple of bottles of gin and a carton of cigarettes."

"Yeah?" He smiled. "I could've gotten into it." He looked down at her body, the long legs stretching out from her narrow hips. He passed his hand over the firm cheeks of her butt.

"I know." She smiled and moved closer. Her nipples pressed against his chest.

On Monday, when Manny checked out of the hotel, the clerk had a message for him—an address on a piece of plain white paper that was stapled to a pink telephone slip.

"I'll be back for my bags," he told the clerk and handed him a five. He didn't know the address specifically, but knew it was just a few blocks away and consequently, it wouldn't be the kind of place to take afternoon tea. He was right. It turned out to be a nude dance theater. Inside it was dark, grimy. The ticket seller who doubled as ticket taker—a bleached blond woman, about sixty—sat unhappily behind a dirty glass shield.

"Eight dollars," she said, not looking up.

"You have an envelope or something, for a stranger?"

She looked up at him, squinted her eyes to see through the smudged glass in the dark theater lobby.

"Twenty-five dollars," she said.

Manny fished out crumpled bills from his jeans pocket, found the right combination of green, and slid it through the little slot.

30

"Looks like you won a free trip to Mexico, kiddo." She opened the door and handed him an empty envelope. "That's all I know. Puerto Vallarta," she said dryly.

"That's it. No who, when, why, where, and how?"

She put the money in her handbag and didn't answer or even look back up.

He looked down. The addressee was the theater. The return address, in Mexico, had been scratched out, but in such a way that it was still decipherable. He put his hand inside the envelope again and found a business card tucked in the corner. A travel agency.

"Such a big envelope?" He looked at the cashier.

"It came that way. I don't touch nothing. No questions. Just what I'm told."

"Show any good?" Manny asked, nodding to dirty, black velvet draperies beyond the turnstile. For Manny, the dark, the mysterious, and the sleazy held no small attraction.

"Eight dollars and you can find out," she said.

He thought again about checking out the show, maybe sipping on a pint of tequila and watching the women take their clothes off. Down and dirty. But he'd told Grayson he'd be there at noon. Besides, the girls in this establishment weren't likely candidates for a *Playboy* centerfold. So for the good of the cause, whatever the hell that was, he'd shove off.

"I like boys," Manny said to her, trying out his new disguise.

"Take a right and down two blocks," she said, not looking up.

"Thanks, sweetie, see ya 'round the pool." Manny's eyes smarted in the sunlight.

5   Manny found Zachary's place comfortable and Zachary himself a likeable guy. Manny was being introduced to some of the best coffee he'd ever had. He experienced the most incredible food and was beginning to understand the subtleties of seasoning and the differences in wine. Manny had even begun to read, something he hadn't done since college. Judging by Zachary's library, there were enough books to last Manny for a millenium or two.

The two of them hit it off pretty well. Zachary never seemed to demand anything of his young housemate and was never intrusive. Sometimes Zachary would fix dinner. Sometimes he'd take Manny to one of the many fine San Francisco restaurants—large ones, small ones, some that looked like they should be closed by the board of health and others secretly tucked away from tourists.

Zachary picked up the tab with the excuse that it was part of his business. He would write it off anyway, he said. At least one night a week they'd go see a film. Sometimes they would stop somewhere and have a drink. It wasn't a bad life, Manny thought. A trifle unexciting perhaps, but the sheets were clean, the towels were fresh.

The only thing that made Manny a little edgy was the wait between instructions. What was he was supposed to be doing about Zachary Grayson? Manny had gone to the travel agency. A woman who wasn't very subtle about her interest in him gave Manny a date to return for his tickets.

For some strange reason, he decided Zachary would go to Mexico, too. It wasn't in the instructions, but so what? He didn't have any real instructions anyway. He rationalized that as a traveling companion, Zachary would make good cover. Besides, the tickets were free. He wanted to do something nice for the guy; and Grayson definitely needed a little adventure in his life.

Manny's initial fears about having to parry sexual innuendos or fend off actual sexual advances diminished each day until midway through the third week, he found himself more than a little teed off that Zachary didn't find him attractive enough to make a pass.

Manny did manage another rendezvous with Suzie, which helped him retrieve, in a bizarre way, a little of his sexual self-image. They met at her place for two hours in the afternoon while her young, blond hunk was rehearsing in a band.

"You're putting on a little weight," Suzie said, watching Manny coming out of the shower. "Somebody's taking pretty good care of you, Brad."

Manny looked down and noticed that his normally flat stomach protruded a bit.

"I've got a sugar daddy," he said. "I guess I need a little exercise," he told her, dropping the towel and moving to the bed. She put her hand on his belly.

"My Buddha," she said, her fingers tracing circles around his navel. "I can make a wish." Her hand moved down.

"Yeah, but can you make it come true?"

"Yes. Watch. It's magic."

"Wait. What if he comes home?" Manny asked.

"I'll cry rape and you're on your own."

"You love him?"

"In my way. He's young. He's got a lot to learn." She lay back on the bed and Manny crawled in next to her, letting his hands go from her breasts down across her belly.

"And me?" Manny asked. "Have I got a lot to learn?"

"You're perfect," Suzie said, allowing her lips to touch his. She brought her leg up over him, the smooth inner thigh warm against his sex. "You don't even know why you're perfect, do you?"

He was pretty sure he didn't want to know. "Why don't you just let me imagine why. I've got a fragile ego and I don't want any illusions shattered. Okay?" He tried to kiss her, but her smiling lips retreated.

"You're perfect because you'll disappear again."

"That's good, I guess."

"Very good." She kissed him. Her fingers found what they were searching for and closed around it. "No expectations. No guilt. No complications," she said. "I like that in a man."

Zachary's friend and neighbor, Leslie, was the first to notice the change in Zachary's attitude and believed he knew why.

"You realize, of course," Leslie told Zachary on the phone—though a person-to-person, in-the-flesh conversation was only a few feet away—"that you have a lilt in your walk."

"A what?" Zachary said.

"A lilt. I've watched you galavanting up and down the hills, my friend, and there's a spring in your step and, dear me, I am so jealous of what put it there."

"Leslie . . ."

"But you deserve it. I was beginning to doubt whether you had a libido. How many years has it been?"

Zachary concluded the conversation without having to say much, which, considering Leslie, wasn't a difficult accomplishment. But the call did trigger the realization that he'd been happier lately. After so many years of cooking for himself or for Leslie—when he could bear hours of soliloquy—he enjoyed trying out his profession on someone whose mouth stopped talking long enough to enjoy food.

Zachary was pleased that Manny didn't pry or preach. And though he was curious, Zachary respected Manny's apparently closeted past. Yes, he found the young man attractive and he assumed that he was gay; but Zachary was actually pleased that sex had not become an issue. He was more than content to appreciate beauty from a distance. And Zachary was flattered, though hardly thrilled, at Manny's increasing insistence that they go off to Mexico together.

If Zachary had not interfered in Manny's coming and goings, the opposite was no longer true. Manny had already intervened in Zachary's predictable life. At the end of weeks of Manny's Mexico lobbying effort, Zachary found himself committed to a flight to Mexico leaving the next day. Manny made the arrangements through some fly-by-night travel agency near the Tenderloin. Zachary agreed to pick up the tickets if Manny would consent to a send-off dinner with Leslie.

Leslie, perhaps kiddingly, perhaps not, had threatened to tell one of the local gay newspapers of the famous cookbook author's new beau unless Zachary agreed to the dinner.

"I think it's time you were outed! Before you're dead," Leslie said, then, as an afterthought, added, "Poor Malcolm Forbes. I would have invited him to dinner had I known. Now *you* must come and have dinner. And you must bring Manny. He'll learn to love me."

About the Mexico trip, Leslie was less encouraging. In fact, he spent two hours trying to talk Zachary out of it. Disease, terrible little microbes in the water, the heat, the humidity, the bandits, the corruption. When Leslie finally saw his arguments were having no effect, he sighed and said: "Well, it's an adventure."

Adventure was precisely what Zachary spent his life avoiding. However, though he had many of the same reservations that Leslie did, Zachary, after half a bottle of sherry, had promised Manny. There was no stopping it now.

Zachary stopped to pick up the tickets. He should have known it would be something like this. Blue-green indoor-outdoor carpet and desk tops as thin as shelf paper.

"What have I gotten myself into?" Zachary asked himself.

"You must be Zach," she said, her voice rasping of a heavy cigarette habit and her violet eyelids slowing from a flutter.

"And you're Linda," Zachary said. "Manny said I should ask for you." He looked around. There was no one else there anyway. In fact, there was no sign of life, past or present, anywhere. Zachary wondered how they paid the rent.

Her giggle had a husky quality. Zachary was thankful. Girlish, high-pitched giggles pierced his brain.

"I have your and Mr. Manning's tickets in the vault." She started away from the desk, then stopped. "I just got back from Portugal. Here." She handed him a worn matchbook with a picture of a male and female dancer silhouetted in some frozen, tortured tango.

Zachary listened patiently to the all-too-detailed description of her trip and the suggestion that he would enjoy Lisbon as much as she did.

"But you'll love Puerto Vallarta, too. I just know you will. So will Mr. Manning. He's crazy, isn't he? I've never seen such green eyes," she said dreamily.

"Yes, his eyes are very green."

"I had a cat once with eyes like that," she said. "He always seemed to be up to something. But I could never figure out just what."

She stared at him, waiting for a comment, perhaps for Zachary to provide some additional insight. At least that's how Zachary saw it. But even if Zachary knew something he wouldn't have told her.

"Cats are very independent animals," Zachary said to break the silence. "One owns them less than they own their owners."

She allowed an uncomprehending laugh to escape. "I'll get your tickets."

Manny knew he was a little out of control. But if those bastards at the company knew everything, why the fuck did they need him? And what was the point of this one-way conversation? He didn't know what he was supposed to do. Was Zachary Grayson some sort of counter-intelligence agent? If so, what was he up to? Was he dangerous? Manny had no idea. Certainly the company didn't bother to clue him in.

Even so, Manny was becoming increasingly nervous about having added Zachary to his travel plans. He had to remind himself that the food writer would be good protection. A younger man traveling with his sugar daddy wasn't what people would expect from the company as standard cover. Besides, Manny reminded himself, he liked the guy. He figured Grayson needed to get out and live a little.

Sending Grayson over to the travel agency was a way to get him out of his apartment for a predictable length of time, giving Manny a chance to look around, something he probably should have done before. Manny chuckled as he went through Grayson's bureau—acting as a careful professional, putting each item back exactly as he found it. He imagined that's how a seasoned pro would do it.

Nothing. Manny went to Grayson's office. Went through his files, his books. He thumbed through the journals, speed-reading for some clue to Grayson's secret existence. Pretty boring stuff. Dinner parties, wine tastings, restaurant notes. If Zachary Grayson was an operative, he was either inactive or damned good. As far as Manny could tell, Grayson had only one friend and even that friendship wasn't exactly close according to the journals.

My next-door neighbor, Leslie, or "Lezzlie" as he prefers to be called (saying it is pronounced like lesbian) is a chubby homosexual in his mid- to late-fifties. Silver curly hair topples over his forehead, chins topple toward his sternum. Despite his roly-poly physique, he is light on his feet, moves quickly and gracefully, quite like his speech.

The entry was dated August 12, 1980. The most recent entry was:

Dear Diary:

I'll probably never stop addressing you as "dear diary." It has the sort of high schoolishness appropriate for such a per-

sonal and petty tome, written to collect the names and dates for later gloating, sobbing, or other embarassment . . . a comfort for me in my waning years, no doubt. What, then, do I call these you may ask. True. It seems I've begun my waning years edging ever closer to the half-century mark.

If I were Gide, I would call this thing a journal, not a diary. As it is, I expect no publication of these shallow, self-indulgent ramblings. It is unlikely there will be any scholarly cry for the journals of Zachary what's-his-name who wrote: Pacific Nouvelle: California Cooking, *even though it sold 200,000 hardbacks. It's already post trend. So there's a gloat and a sob.*

Ah, but the reason for opening these sacred pages. Manny, who has entered my life as some sort of electric shock therapy, has convinced me to go to Puerto Vallarta. He tells me it is for my own good. That I need "an adventure," that my complexion has a "milky" (he meant sickly) look, which is no doubt uncomplimentary to my sagging chest and growing paunch (a professional medal, I tell him since I am both a cook and a writer in whatever order one chooses). He is right, of course. I could use the sun and exercise.

The truth of the matter is that Manny has some inexplicable, desperately immediate business to handle, I suspect. What a strange fellow.

Enough for now. It's time for the recipe for profiteroles stuffed with mousse of smoked salmon. Not my idea of breakfast fare.

P.S. Poor Manny will have to endure this evening with Leslie. More later.

—Z

"Boy, this is dangerous stuff. I sure hope the KGB doesn't get hold of this," Manny said out loud.

Maybe Zachary made contact at one of his regular haunts. A waiter or bartender or clerk in a bookstore. Maybe in China-town. Manny closed the diary and put it back exactly where he'd gotten it, making sure the angle on the shelf was the same. Zachary had to be connected to the operation somehow. Otherwise, he wouldn't have gotten the dossier and instructions to "get close" to him. Yet Manny's only clear mission was again that of courier. Pick up something from someone and come back to San Francisco.

6 At the dinner party, Leslie greeted the guests at the door, offering Manny his limp hand by way of greeting. They had met; however, Leslie hadn't made a favorable impression on Manny. Leslie, on the other hand, seemed to find Manny an object of amusement.

"Am I supposed to shake it or kiss it?" Manny asked.

"Tsk, tsk," Leslie lisped with enthusiastic affectation. "This is going to be fun. Just a gentle squeeze, Manny," he said extending his arm again. "Your virility isn't in question . . . at the moment."

Leslie whirled around the couch. "Have a seat, boys. This is Fassir, my very own Arabic millionaire—or are you Turkish? Never mind, it's all the same. Manny, can you appreciate twenty-five-year-old scotch? It would be quite past its prime for Fassir, but I see you appreciate vintage. For you, Zach, the usual? Rum and tonic, twist of lemon? One can tell so much about a person by what he drinks. Anyway, sit down.

"Sorry for the new design," Leslie continued with a dramatic sweep around his recently redone apartment. "It's not very comfortable. I lost my mind. I admit it. I had a crush on this Zen Buddhist and before I knew it, I hadn't a comfortable chair in the house."

"Perhaps you should have hired an Arab," Fassir said. "Then you would have had tons of pillows to languish on."

Leslie prepared drinks while continuing his monologue.

"I do so love to languish. *Languish.* The word is absolutely erotic. People have lost the language, you know. There's no appreciation of quality. There's just no such thing as first class anymore. Except Fassir, of course. He accepts nothing but. He is in search of not only life, but of perfection, if in no other way than his obsessive, and very successful pursuit of masculine beauty. Is 'masculine' the right word? No, of course it isn't. Feminine isn't right either. Neither is hermaphroditic. It's . . ."

Leslie handed Zachary and Manny drinks. Fassir squirmed.

"Androgenous," Leslie said as if he had just won a game-show prize. "Yes, that's the word. Fassir has the eye and skill to find and pluck these boys at precisely the right moment, don't you, Fassir, before even a hint of a bruise, and then is so clever as to taste it only once because he recognizes the decay his own delicate touch has introduced. I am continually amazed."

"I, too, am amazed," Fassir said, handing Leslie his glass for a refill. "It's so refreshing to see a man of your power and years so capable of awe."

The conversational tone set for the evening, the four men followed a waiter of no more than seventeen to the balcony. They stood at the railing as the quiet, handsome young Latino named Arturo finished setting the table for a starlit dinner.

"Case in point, this boy. This beauty," Leslie said. "Fassir has lent me Arturo for the evening. Absolutely delightful." Then looking down toward the bay, "I do believe this is the only way to see the wharf—at a considerable distance." Leslie pointed to the twinkling lights below. "Whatever do people see in that place? I'm such a snob, I love it. Let's sit down. And don't let me do all the talking. I shall have a plate full of cold food while you're having your after-dinner drinks if I'm not careful. Oh, and I promise, Zach—no Mexican food. You'll have enough of that on the first day. I don't know how you're going to deal with that, with your sensitive palate. What we do for love. Why on earth Puerto Vallarta? Good night to Mexico, I say. Just good night to it." He waved his hands as if they could dismiss a country the way a lord would dismiss a servant.

The dinner progressed civilly at first. Leslie ate, as he promised. Manny and Fassir exchanged observations on the Mideast. At Manny's coaching, Fassir did most of the talking. However, one of Manny's remarks about developing countries freed Leslie from the tiresome task of remaining quiet.

"Since you are so concerned about the plight of the Third World," Leslie said, swallowing quickly, his fork clunking down onto the china, "it seems a bit odd, doesn't it, Manny, that you should enjoy such a high style through the kindness of strangers and then spend two leisurely weeks on the beaches of Puerto Vallarta? I assume you'll be taking food to the poor, caring for the sick?"

"You have some extra beluga and Dom Perignon I can take them?" Manny asked, bringing the napkin to his lips and shoving his plate away.

"Put all those little revolutionaries in control and you think all will be well? No, the new generals will be sitting here like this. Fat and happy. The current fat cats will sit in prison cells fighting for roaches and a moldy tortilla and espousing reform until they pull off a coup. You just don't get it, do you?"

"You are much too wise for me, Leslie," Manny said, smiling. "You've come up with a world view that can give you greed and gluttony without guilt. Congratulations."

"Guilt. Guilt, Manny? Guilt was manufactured by those who wish to keep others oppressed. It is all part of the plan to keep people in philosophical ignorance, the plot of popes and mothers everywhere." Leslie laughed, his second chin bouncing in syncopation with his belly. "It's to keep everyone asking those foolish questions. Who am I? Where am I going? What am I doing here?"

"Who are you, Leslie?"

"Who am I? Where am I going? What am I doing here? What's it all about?" He shook his head. "Wrong questions. The real question is what do I want. How do I get it? How do I keep it? When are you going to play with the big boys, Manny? When? We humans are not so different from the rest of the animal species, are we? We are all fighting to keep our territories, to get our food. And there is not one honest soul out there who—either given the right opportunity or backed against the wall—wouldn't do whatever is necessary to survive. What's it all about, Manny? It's about staying alive until we die. It's eating, sleeping, defecating, and having sex. It's about not becoming bored, keeping what you have, and getting more until you die. And that's it. Then you become fertilizer for the cornfields in Indiana."

Manny, after taking a sip of wine, turned to Zachary.

"Is it true that baby Leslie's first words were 'When's brunch?' "

46

Manny was surprised when Leslie laughed.

"I think that's probably true," he said, "I'm the one from whom the stereotype was taken. But what I want to know is what in God's name do you two see in each other?"

"I was about to ask Zach the same question about you," Manny said, managing to keep his tone a wee bit short of contempt.

"Leslie merely likes lively dinner conversation," Zachary said. "I've heard him argue just as passionately for Mother Teresa. It's all theater."

"What do I see in Zachary?" Leslie asked picking up on the question with delight. "I'd love to answer. Zach brings me pleasure," Leslie said, calming. "He leadeth me beside fine wines. He engageth me in intelligent conversation, though I must provide the brilliant parts. And he provideth me with the all too occasional company of striking things like you, Manny. He is as much of a god as I ever expect to have." Leslie dabbed the corners of his mouth with the napkin and turned toward Zachary. "But Zach, now I need more. It's time for you to account for yourself. Come out from behind your writer's grist-for-the-mill objectivity."

"Don't confuse me with fiction writers, Leslie. The only grist I have is what's on the plate," Zachary said, looking down at his food.

Leslie scooted his chair back, looked up at the sky. "Let me play grand inquisitor. With Manny's help, we have established that I am some sort of greedy dinosaur. Fassir is a classic pagan and could care less what anybody else does. Manny, of course, is on the difficult road to saintdom. More wine, Manny? Or are you on a gallant crusade, fighting for peace and killing for equality?"

"Actually, I believe I simply become whatever is convenient for your purpose." Leslie smiled.

"Enough about you. We need to know where you stand, Zach. We staunch believers, of whatever stripe, consider those who refuse to declare an allegiance one way or another to be either against us or in the way."

"Probably in the way," Zachary replied.

"You don't care about piling up money?"

"I have more than enough. I am comfortable."

"What about power?"

"I don't care about it."

"What about the huddled masses, yearning to breathe free?"

"I wish them all the luck in the world," Zachary said, tiring of the game.

"You have no political, religious beliefs?"

"My grandmother," Zachary said, picking up his fork, "refused to talk about sex, politics, or religion."

"So you just write your books and live your comfortable life with no driving message for the world?"

"Don't overcook your vegetables," Zachary said, taking a bite of asparagus.

"And what would you kill for, Zach? Don't tell me love."

"All right, I won't."

"Come now, it's clear, Zach. I would kill for money and power. Manny would kill for a noble cause. Fassir would kill for a blossom. A ruthless artist. Artists are the most dangerous, because you must be able to see with their eyes to know if you're the victim."

"You have nothing to fear, Leslie," Fassir said.

"So, you see, unless someone wants to debate my characterization of them . . . do you, Manny?"

"No."

"You, Fassir?"

"I wouldn't dare."

"Then dear, dear Zachary, what would you kill for? Or are you truly one of those passive ones? The Gandhi of Russian Hill?" Then, noticing Zachary putting a piece of veal in his mouth, "Oh, but you do eat meat, don't you?"

"I try to, Leslie," he said, putting his fork down, swallowing, and taking a sip of wine.

"You must tell me what you'd kill for," Leslie pressed.

"A cigarette and a cup of espresso."

"Arturo," Leslie said. Arturo nodded and disappeared. "I'm not going to accept these attempts to change the subject, Zachary. Is there any situation that could cause you to take someone else's life?"

"Are you recruiting for the Marine Corps?" Manny asked.

"I would if I could get by with it. I could use a few good men." Leslie looked at Manny. "You see, Zachary really could kill—but only something immediate, demanding no thought, just a brief glimpse of passion or fear that lurks in the heart of every one of nature's beasts—even Zachary, even the most civilized, the most cerebral."

Leslie pushed himself still further back from the table, got up, and went to the balcony.

"You could not coldly calculate someone's death. It would have to be a thoughtless act." Leslie turned, the night serving as the scrim for what Manny hoped would be his final performance of the evening. "But no matter how refined you think you are, no matter how far removed from the petty, from the banal, from the vulgar, you *can* kill."

"What's this obsession you have about my killing someone?" Zachary asked.

"That's what I like about you. You've transcended all the animal desires. Well, maybe," Leslie said, looking at Manny. "Life is a movie or a cruise. You'll observe but not participate. You'll not even play shuffleboard. You do not pass judgment, so how could you convict, sentence, punish? But have you no curiosity?"

The tiny cups, filled with strong black coffee, jiggled on Arturo's silver tray as he reappeared on the balcony. The boy automatically proffered a silver sugar bowl and Leslie dropped two heaping teaspoons into the small cup.

"When this takes effect," Leslie said, his lisp becoming more intentional, "I'll be so sweetly charming, even Arturo won't be able to resist me. Isn't that right, Arturo?"

Arturo smiled.

Zachary thought the coffee arrived just in time. It not only stopped Leslie's obsessive discussion of death, it would diminish his own slide into inebriation. Also, Arturo's diplomatic, yet flirtatious grin had warmed Zachary uncomfortably. "The wine was perfect, Leslie."

"Don't change the subject." Leslie took a deep breath. "Oh, let's do change the subject. I have so much fun when it's my party. No one can throw me out."

"We can all leave," Fassir said, winking.

"But not until you've had a glass of port. That would be uncivilized."

"Could I trouble you for some sherry instead?" Zachary asked.

"Sherry? Dear Zachary. Sherry is for the ladies. While we gentlemen sip port and smoke cigars, the ladies adjourn to the parlor and gossip and giggle with their glasses of sherry."

"I'll pass on the cigars as well. I'll just go into the other room and giggle with the girls," Zachary said, getting up.

50

"Well said." Leslie crumpled his napkin, tossing it on his half-finished plate of food. "Let's let Fassir and Manny have their little summit on Middle Eastern affairs while we go in the other room and talk about draperies like good homosexuals."

7 Zachary didn't want to wait until morning to finish packing. He couldn't get to sleep unless he was sure he had not forgotten the various elements of his rituals—the tobacco, ink for his fountain pen. And there was the question of the right clothes about which he was pretty much at a loss. Did it get cool at night? Would he need a sweater? Could he get his clothes laundered there?

Though Leslie and others thought him to be a reasonably erudite individual, Zachary knew otherwise. He had little real knowledge of geography, climates. If he had investigated Mexican cuisine at any length, he might have understood a bit of the culture, but he had not really gotten around to Spanish or Central and South American food in any depth, preferring American, French, Italian, and all of the varieties of Asia. In fact, he knew more about North African cuisine than he did about Mexican.

The idea that he would be completely at Manny's mercy in all regards including language was a little frightening. Traveling all that way with a virtual stranger certainly was the undertaking of a fool.

"I'd pack cotton or nylon," Manny said. He leaned against the doorway of the bedroom. "Something you can wash out and hang up to dry."

Zachary wondered how long he'd been there, watching. He hoped not for long. It was embarrassing to be watched fussing about his things like some maiden aunt.

"I don't have anything like that," Zachary said. "Did you enjoy yourself this evening?"

"You have curious friends," Manny said.

"I should think they felt the same way about you."

"I'm sure they did. What does Leslie do for a living?"

"He told me he clips coupons," Zachary said. "When he first told me I thought he meant those bits of paper people take to the supermarket."

Manny laughed.

"I'm afraid," Zachary continued, "the world of high finance is as strange to me as most of the rest of the world."

"And Fassir? White slave trade, maybe?"

"Oil, I think. Oil related anyway," Zachary replied, noticing Manny was more than a little sloshed.

"These are your friends?" Manny asked, handing Zachary a stack of underwear.

Zachary was quiet for a moment.

"I don't know," he said. "Perhaps. Leslie is concerned about my welfare. I believe that. I believe there must be something beneath the clownish exterior—a substance that we all have behind the defenses. I'm sure you do, too."

"You might be surprised, Zach," Manny said, disappearing from the doorway.

54

8 "How old are you really, Bat?" Sali had been uncomfortable when Bat paid him the nightly visit to request a favor. Tonight he was comfortable. He enjoyed the small place the old man rented behind the jewelry store. He enjoyed the smell of wood and tea. After they had talked for a while and listened to Coltrane and Miles Davis, Sali had finally asked the question he'd longed to ask.

"It doesn't matter, does it? How old you are tells you nothing. How old are you, Sali?"

"I don't know."

"See, you are lucky not to be bound by time. In some ways you are as old as me." The old man held a stringless mandolin, his long, bent fingers forcing a small piece of sandpaper over its neck, occasionally stopping to let his bare fingers feel the grain of the wood. "So I don't need to know anyway, any more than I need to know what you look like. I know you. I used to be so sad being blind, but now I think that having sight is a handicap. When I could see, I often couldn't get past the glitter . . . or the deformity. Now, after many years I have begun to hear the heart, rather than be beguiled by the packaging."

"People in town say you are over a hundred."

"Could be. I stopped counting a long time ago. Once I tried to figure it out. But I couldn't. I don't even remember what year I moved to Mexico anymore or when it was that we met."

"You started teaching me English three years ago, I think."

"Was it?" Bat said without a trace of surprise.

"You're right, it doesn't matter."

"Sali, you must be careful."

Sali left the old man, cut through the quiet, late night streets to his place—an abandoned sewer supervisor's office on a muddy slope where the polluted river met the ocean.

The concrete block structure was crumbling and inside, the decor consisted of a small lantern to read by, a mat to sleep on, a blanket to sleep under, and a large, jagged piece of mirror to look into. And look into it he did—sometimes in admiration and sometimes just to reassure himself that he existed.

If it was too cold, Sali was welcome at Bat's, where he could sleep next to a fire. Tonight, Sali was tired, but he felt good. His visits to the old man always calmed his body and excited his brain, made him think of things that made him wonder at the world rather than being bitter about it.

Bat had introduced him to English, to jazz, and most recently to the guitar. Unfortunately, he had no patience for it and declined Bat's gift of a beautiful, handmade instrument, explaining that he had nowhere to keep it. He didn't like to own things. If he owned something, he would always worry about it being stolen as he worried now about that strange little object Bat had given him, the thing Sali was to deliver tomorrow.

He slipped off his clothes, then put the lantern next to the mirror. Sometimes he wished he looked more mature, but then many of the male *touristas* liked him the way he was. Despite the police and many of the townspeople, he enjoyed the way he made a living. Unlike some of the other boys, Sali went with those people he liked and if they'd get rude once the deal was struck, he would leave, usually taking something of value for his trouble.

He wondered what Bat would think if he knew. He probably did know. Bat didn't concern himself with such things, the youth concluded.

He went back to the mat, put out the warm flame of the lantern. In darkness, the night sky now appeared in window. Soon, perhaps dreams would come from the stars, enter his room and inhabit his sleeping mind.

It was too hot for the blanket and a breeze whisked across his nakedness. He slid his hands down his body. It would help him sleep.

I suspect we are somewhere over Arizona. Manny is asleep by the window. I am envious. I cannot sleep on planes, even though last night I could only manage three or four hours of sleep and those were punctuated by disturbing dreams. Perhaps if I lived an exciting life, I'd have boring dreams. I hope I didn't scare Manny too much. He woke me up, said I was screaming. He looked worried and brought me a glass of milk. I don't know why his concern surprised me.

Early flights should be illegal. So should bon-voyage dinners. Manny and Fassir seemed to have gotten along well, though I detected some intense mental jousting. Was I ever that competitive? Actually, no.

—Z

Manny fidgeted, then sat up straight, looking out of the window.

"Not quite heaven," Manny said, "but we're getting close."

"You're alive," Zachary said, closing his journal.

"Among the living. How about you?"

"I assume so, but I'm never quite sure."

"Are you sure of anything?" Manny asked.

"You're referring to the dinner conversation?" Zachary sighed in unpleasant recollection. "My passionless soul. That's something you and Leslie agree on, I take it?"

"Well, you're not really alive, are you?"

"I breathe," Zachary said matter-of-factly. "I am often amused. But I'm not in pain."

"Anesthetized, maybe."

"I appreciate passion, Manny. I appreciate growth, grace, beauty. Perhaps it is a shame to find them more readily in books and plays. . . ." Zachary felt a bit irritated by Manny's uncharacteristically rude questions and decided to set him back a bit. "But what about all this business with Leslie? Do you mind that he and Fassir think you are a kept boy? That you sleep with me?"

"Who gives a shit?"

"You don't care?"

"I'm in and out of people's lives so quick . . ." Manny stopped short. He realized two things: If he wasn't careful he'd give away the store, and that he was about to share an intimacy. "Does it bother you?"

"No," Zachary said. "I enjoy it. It saves me from the condescending pity he gives me when he thinks my sex life is unsatisfactory."

"It is unsatisfactory, isn't it?"

58

·It is quite satisfactory."

"You have one, then?"

"No, that's why it is satisfactory."

"I don't buy it, kiddo," Manny said.

"You have a purpose, it seems, though God knows what it is. It doesn't matter, you're entertaining." Zachary rarely intended to hurt, but Manny was probing where he had no business probing. This time, he intended to sting.

"I entertain you?" Manny asked, now only half-smiling.

"Yes," Zachary said grinning, "though perhaps amusing is a better word."

"Thanks, toots."

"Furthermore, I am using you," Zachary said.

"Thanks again."

"Don't mention it."

Manny pulled out the in-flight magazine and perused the pages with obvious disinterest.

"And you are using *me,* aren't you?" Zachary added after a few minutes had passed.

Manny went pale. His voice broke when he spoke. "How is that?"

"What is an actor without an audience?"

"Oh," Manny said, relieved. "I guess so."

Puerto Vallarta was smaller than Zachary imagined—at least the town proper. Manny had already booked a room in a hotel in the center of town, having heard it had been a hang-out for film director John Huston.

"Huston's dead," Zach told him.

"Maybe we can get his room then." Manny smiled.

The room they did get overlooked the main street, a wide

59

promenade which ran along the ocean where quaint light posts and picture-perfect palms preceded both the beach and the Pacific.

Manny hung up his few clothes with what Zachary perceived as reckless abandon. "I need a drink," Manny said.

Zachary went into the bathroom, tested for hot water. Satisfied, he intended to lay back on the bed and take a nap. The trip from the airport in Mazatlán to the small town Liz and Dick made famous was anything but restful.

The plane was late. They'd missed the regular bus connection. That meant a smoldering, dusty ride in a windowless van. The seat springs rose in anarchy and the truck's shocks no longer absorbed the rude ruts in the road.

No way, Zach informed his brain, would he endure a replay on the way back.

"C'mon, don't poop out on me," Manny said. "I've got a delivery to make, then I'll come back and we can check out the town. It won't take long."

After Manny left, Zachary ordered up a soft drink. The bottle was warm. The youth who brought it apologized and returned a few minutes later with a chunk of ice and an ice pick. Zachary tipped the boy, and took the ice and the pick to the bathroom sink. He remembered the warnings about the water and drank the soda warm.

Despite the fact that he and Manny did more than tour the town when he got back, Zachary felt the need to keep at least a portion of his ritual alive. Before turning off the lamp beside his bed, Zachary pulled out his diary, adjusted his glasses, and removed the cap of his Mont Blanc.

Dear Diary:

An agonizing day. A strange evening. I've never seen Manny quite so nervous. He spilled a bottle of red wine on his white slacks. It's a shame they weren't spoiled by a better wine. Poor boy's mind was elsewhere. Then a telephone call. And a rather defensive reply to my no-more-than-casual curiosity. Who would call at that late hour? He's quite right. It wasn't any of my business. Perhaps tomorrow will be better. I've brought along Isherwood's On a Visit Down There. *It seems the appropriate time to re-read one of my all-time favorites. Tomorrow the beach and genuine leisure.*

Zach, Puerto Vallarta

9 Shaken, Sali awoke. He took a sudden and involuntary gulp of salt air.

"Where is it, kid?" came the voice of a very large man sitting beside the youth on the very small bed. When Sali didn't answer, a fat hand came to rest on the youth's thigh. The boy could feel the heat through the light blanket.

"Where is it, Sali?" The man's face was carved from rock. At least fifty, Sali thought, with the shoulders of a bulldozer. "Listen to me," the man said, pulling out a pack of unfiltered Pall Malls, lighting one while he spoke. "We're not talking about your peddling some hot passports so a few of your *compadres* can make it to the promised land. We're not talking about swiping some poor shnook's wallet or copping a few joints. We're talking deep shit."

The hand moved. Earl Patrick's fingers held the boy's testicles in a vice-like grip.

Sali, curling in pain, bent toward his captor. His teeth

found the flesh of the man's forearm and bit—deep. Sali pulled back like a dog trying to rip meat from the bone.

The man, emanating a loud, gutteral sound sprang to his feet, then fell backward over the lantern. Sali reached beneath his pillow, grabbed the small item, much smaller and thinner than a dime, and raced—brown, slender, and completely naked—through the quiet, early-morning streets of Puerto Vallarta.

He could still feel the dull pain in his groin as his legs carried him across the sand, down the beach.

He didn't look back. It would slow him down. He didn't know if he was being followed or, if at this moment, his back was held in the sight of a gun. The little metallic, coin-like object in hand, Sali angled toward the ocean, running below the watermark so the tide would erase his footprints. Now he turned and ran the opposite way so that he would not be followed.

Ocean spray danced against his body. His thin shadow crossed the morning's light. He noticed the sand glitter pink and gray as the waves retreated.

Sali was scared, but he was never happier. This was freedom. Naked. Running. His life on the edge. Nothing was more exciting, exhilerating, than this freedom of his.

Manny was still asleep when Zachary awoke at his usual early hour. He went to the window and smiled, seeing, instead of the usual prison in the gray dawn, the palm trees he had thought about weeks ago. The smile seemed to fade away, though, and the pleasant irony he felt at the sight made him uneasy.

Perhaps it was just the lack of familiarity that made him feel that way. Ritual interruptus, he thought. Nevertheless, he sensed something ominous behind the pink sky, the sticky warmth of the air and the constant drone of the ceiling fan.

He plucked one of his hand-rolled cigarettes from the tin and lit it. Without coffee, the tobacco tasted harsh and dry. He stamped it against the bottom of the ashtray, content to watch the little stream of smoke trail up and be chopped and dispersed by the ceiling fan.

Sali walked at the water's edge, sometimes having to wade waist-high, until he reached a deserted beach. This brief stretch of undeveloped shore lay between the town beaches and the hotel beaches. Sali encountered no one. It was still early, too early for even a stray tourist.

He walked back into the squat trees and bushes. He foraged the low undergrowth for something to conceal his nakedness. He found the stained remnant of a red satin dress, tore it into a manageable size and, through a process of tying and folding, fashioned something with the cut of a bathing suit.

"Not too bad," he said to himself. He ran his palm across the cheeks of his ass, feeling the smoothness of the satin. He smiled and wished he had a mirror.

Sali picked up the little piece of metal. Without markings, it didn't seem as valuable as a single peso. He held it up to the sun. He couldn't see through it, had no idea what it was or why anybody wanted it. But somebody did. Apparently more than one somebody and he was pretty sure the burly bastard who grabbed his nuts wasn't the one he was supposed to give it to. Of that, Sali was quite sure.

He slid the silver piece into the crotch of his newly formed swimsuit. The boy sighed and looked around. He would spend the day at the beach and come back here to sleep. Surely, mid-

65

day at the public beach would be safe. He would not keep his appointment. Too dangerous. Another time. Another place, perhaps.

Manny and Zachary planned to go for a morning swim—though morning was nearly over and only Manny got in the water. They'd had a very late, very lazy breakfast of *huevos rancheros,* a term Manny said sounded like a battle cry.

They ate at the hotel on a small balcony overlooking the ocean and the main promenade.

"Huevos rancheros!" Manny screamed over the balcony, causing the tourists below to stop and gape. "Geronimo!" Manny's behavior in Mexico, as attested to last night, was unpredictable and often embarrassing. Zachary, however, found it endearing. He envied Manny's ability to let go. Then again, there seemed to be a little desperation in his antics. In any event, Zachary considered himself far too stuffy for his own good.

Manny spent the remainder of breakfast complaining about the musicians who seemed to follow them from bar to bar last night as if it were their assigned task to irritate him personally.

"It was the trumpet," Manny said, "the fucking trumpet that drove me mad. I felt like shoving that piece of brass down his throat."

"You did," Zach said.

"I didn't."

"Well, nearly. I had to give him at least five million pesos."

"You lie," Manny laughed.

"There were a lot of pesos changing hands. Too many for me to count."

"I won't pay you five million pesos."

66

"Forget it. Only please, Manny, don't try to fix me up with the natives."

"I didn't."

"Fortunately, the man didn't speak English."

At 2 P.M., Manny stood in front of the bathroom mirror, preparing himself for another private venture into some part of the city. Zachary made notes in his diary.

Manny is nervous. At first I thought it was just being in an exotic land and he was letting loose a bit. On second thought, however, I believe it has something to do with whatever business it is that he has here. Maybe he is saying good-bye to a lover. Perhaps my ascribing a secret tryst to these strange and sudden departures merely means that my imagination is more interesting than the real story. Then again, perhaps my imagination is very poor compared to the real story. Good lord, I hope he's not involved in the drug business. That's certainly something I hadn't thought about, poor naive fool that I am. It is certainly something I had better think about. Dear lord, let it be a love tryst!

Zach, Puerto Vallarta

After Manny left, Zachary went to the mirror. He looked at himself carefully. He wasn't worried about the lines, which like a fine spider web spun away from his eyes. He didn't mind the growing creases in the neck or even the increasing shapelessness of his body. What he minded was the crease above the bridge of the nose, between the eyebrows. He minded that a great deal. It made him look as if he took life seriously.

He'd have to relax, he told himself. Buy some sunglasses.

Have an adventure. "No," he said to the mirror. The food would be adventure enough.

Zachary avoided the "better" beaches, the ones up by the new hotels, choosing instead one inhabited by the local population. Though the beer was warmer, it was also less expensive. Though the public beach was noisier, the chances were that those who surrounded him would be speaking Spanish. He would not, therefore, be tempted to eavesdrop and could read in relative peace.

He found a chair outside an open beach bar, and though not much of a beer drinker until last night, ordered a Superior, rented an umbrella, and opened his book.

Halfway through the foreword, Zachary sensed a presence. It was a young Mexican boy. Couldn't be more than sixteen. Hair wet and beads of water clinging to his slender chest like opals. The boy in a red swim suit was staring at *him*.

"Yes?" Zachary inquired.

"I am at your service," said the boy. "Anything you want, I can get it for you. Food maybe?"

"Thank you, no. I had a late breakfast." His answer confirmed his recent evaluation of himself—stuffy, formal, cold.

"Something else?" the boy persisted.

"I don't know what that might be. I am really quite content. I appreciate your offer."

"Your fortune, *señor*," the boy said, his eyes looking directly into Zachary's, "I can tell it."

"Ah, you're very versatile."

"Yes," the boy smiled, continuing his intense gaze.

"You speak English very well.

"Yes, that, too. I can do many things. Anything you like."

Zachary felt uncomfortable with the boy's tone. Was he

reading too much into it? "Well," he sputtered. "I don't know. What? You see there's nothing I need. Or want, right now."

"Later. I can come back. Anytime. When you say?"

"Let's see." Zachary managed to stumble through a few *ahs* and *uhs*. He found it very difficult to talk. He felt himself blush. He wasn't sure he wanted the boy to leave. But what was the point? "Perhaps," Zachary continued, his voice still quavering, "just the fortune."

"Only 250 pesos."

"That's fine."

The boy sat on the sand, at Zachary's feet. He reached up and took Zachary's hand, though continuing to look at his eyes.

"You have very kind blue eyes. The brown specks mean you have power. But your palm says you do not use your power. It also says you do not work with your hands."

"But I do. You see this in the lines?"

"No, I feel softness. You do not work with your hands. However, you use a pen or pencil very much."

"Well," Zach said. "Quite true. I don't lay bricks. I'm impressed. You do have occult powers."

"The pen is shown by the callus here."

"Oh," Zachary said with disappointment. It was merely a practical observation. The boy was smart, but so far he had not demonstrated any great occult ability. Too bad. For some reason, Zachary had suddenly wanted to believe.

The boy's fingers moved along Zachary's palm gently, tracing the faint lines. Zachary was increasingly uncomfortable.

"Your life line is split. Here—see?"

"What does that mean? Am I going to die soon?" Zachary felt more comfortable in generalities and felt himself smiling as the youth was about to comment on matters of life and death.

"Not real death, because it begins again. Here." The boy's fingers moved along Zachary's palm. To him it seemed too intimate and Zachary felt himself blushing again. But the boy continued. "It means a big change in your life. A big change."

"What will it be?"

"I do not know. It does not say. This line says you have a child."

"I'm afraid my hand lies then." Zachary smiled. "I have no children."

"Then you will," the boy insisted.

"Not likely," Zachary smiled.

"Your hand does not lie. And I don't lie. Maybe you don't have one now. If you don't, you will."

"When will this important change occur?" Zachary asked.

"Sometime in the middle of your life or maybe soon after the middle of your life. You will live a long time."

Zachary realized, if the youth did not, that he was already in the middle of his life. This "change" would no doubt happen sooner than later.

"And will I be happy in this long life?"

"Depends," the boy said. "This is your love line. You see this? I think when you were very young, someone was very special to you. But that person is gone now. Am I right?"

"Doesn't everyone have at least one person in his life who is important?"

"Maybe. This person was not just important." The boy looked into Zachary's eyes. "Your eyes are wet. It was very sad. I'm sorry to talk about it. You will have someone else. It is in your palm."

10 "You shouldn't have come here," she said. It wasn't an admonition. It was a statement in a bland and expressionless voice. "Now that you are, come in."

Manny followed her through the heavy door into the darkened home. Stale air met his nostrils enough for him to draw back. The windows were heavily draped, perhaps intending to keep out the heat, but trapping it instead.

"What could I do? He wasn't there," Manny said. He trailed after her, through the dining room, dimly lit through slats slightly askew in the shutter frames. An ornate, though not necessarily expensive chandelier hung over a massive Spanish-style dining room table, the top of which was dulled with yellowish dust. The rugs were limp from the humid air.

"They probably got him." Though she was no more than fifty, she walked delicately, as if she were balancing a plate on her head. Hung over, Manny thought. He knew the feeling. He followed her to the kitchen where she pulled a beer from the refrigerator and handed it to Manny. "They know me here, now they'll know you."

She spoke as if it really didn't matter. Manny thought that beyond her hangover, there was nothing. Burnt out.

"They'll think I am a gay tourist traveling with my sugar daddy," he said.

They went into a room that opened out to a walled garden. From the chair he could see a dingy, plastic pelican, one of the seven dwarfs, several ceramic frogs. Foliage, such as it was, swallowed up the little statues, reclaiming the land without interference from the proprietor.

Dead leaves floated in the pool, where a partially inflated, half-submerged, plastic fish lay motionless. Manny couldn't make out the patterns on the lawn chairs. Rain had caked the dust that had gathered into a thin layer of dried mud.

"You shouldn't have called either," she said. Another matter-of-fact statement.

"Well, my company hasn't been sending me to the right seminars. Look, maybe they—whoever the fuck they are— will think I'm your nephew or something, visiting my maiden aunt for her inheritance. Maybe my mother. May I call you 'Mom'?"

"Oh yeah, thanks. I really need that."

"I need a mother."

She didn't laugh. "I've been married—three times. No kids."

"Three times a lady."

"He wanted children, the last one," she looked at Manny. There was a mild hint of accusation in her voice.

"I cook them for breakfast," Manny said.

"What?"

"Children."

She laughed. He had broken through.

"If he's in trouble," she said, "he could be staying with the old black man in town. Blind. Got to be a hundred years old. They're friends. A strange pair." She shook her head. "The old man taught him English. Or he might be hiding at the public beach. Gringos—and it's a big, ugly gringo who generally works this little sandbox—stand out like sore thumbs so he could figure he'd be safe among hundreds of locals. I don't know."

"How will I know the kid?"

"That was the point, you know. He was supposed to know you, so you wouldn't have to come here."

She led him to the door.

"You should get out more often."

"I should grow wings," she said.

Shortly after the boy left, Zachary felt agitated. He wanted to move around, but settled on the renegotiation of the umbrella at an angle to provide the longest possible period of complete shade. Just as he managed to settle into calm and concentration, a mammoth Mexican woman tumbled down the steps of the bar. She came to rest in the sand a few feet away.

At the bar's entrance, several men—the obvious means of her propulsion—gathered. They laughed and cheerfully, drunkenly toasted her with their beer bottles.

The woman, dressed in a black wrap-around dress, must have weighed 250 pounds. Perhaps more. The dress, twisted around her large body like a grotesque rope, no longer covered everything. She apparently was ready for a swim. Beneath her dress was a tiny, magenta triangle. On someone else it would have been a normal bikini. On her, it looked like a g-string.

The woman made several drunken attempts to get up, then

passed out. The Mexicans laughed, gave her one final toast, and went back inside the bar.

Zachary again settled back in his chair. He hoped this distracting bit of absurd theater was over. It wasn't.

The woman lifted her sand-encrusted face and began to inch her way toward the ocean. Slowly, almost instinctively, it seemed, by a strange combination of scoots and rolls, she got to the ocean's edge, where waves nibbled at her feet.

For a moment, Zachary thought he ought to do something. But what could he do with a 250-pound drunk who didn't speak the same language? The water, he thought, would eventually sober her and she would be on her way. He flipped back a page in his book to see if he could make some sense of what he was reading.

A crowd gathered, mostly children selling glazed-eyed, roasted fish mounted on the ends of pointed sticks. The children began shouting, jabbing their sticks toward her as she inched her way toward the water. The waves now lapped at her face. She scooted still farther, then passed out again, bloated and lifeless, waiting, it appeared, for the tide to come take her away.

When the waves came in, they seemed to lift her body and toss it from side to side. When the waves receded again, her body settled. Then the water approached again, teasing. The children screamed and jumped, thrusting the primitive skewers up in the air as if they were spears and they were enacting an ancient tribal ceremony.

A toothless old man came out of the bar and walked down to the woman. Holding her ankles, he dragged her back from the water, cursing her every grunting step of the way. She slept again.

But her dress had opened. The strings of the magenta fabric

74

hung loosely. Walking up brazenly, one of the children pulled away the flap to the cheers, whistles, and applause of the older youths.

Another man came out of the bar, toothless and barely able to walk himself. He yelled at the children. Still laughing, they retreated. The man retied the suit. He made a half-hearted run at the children, yelling, waving his arms, then staggered back into the bar.

Slowly, the children edged back around her, but grew bored at her inert state and went back about their business of selling fish to the people on the beach.

Zachary ordered another beer, lit a cigarette. In a few hours, the beach would be deserted. There would be the promised postcard sunset. The tide would come in still farther.

He looked at the woman. She was moving again—slowly—toward the sea. No one else watched. The water came in farther each time until it penetrated her nostrils. Salt water invaded her eyes and throat. She moved toward the water, choking. The white-frothed tide lifted the woman, her black dress floating ephemerally, silky fins in the foam.

Zachary looked around. There was no one to help her. How *would* one help her? Should he try to prevent her from going where she obviously wanted to go?

The wave that tossed her left as suddenly as it had come. Her body rolled, shook with sputtering, choking coughs. Suddenly she sat upright. The next wave caught her breast-high. It lifted her, but did not bring her down. She sat there defiantly, striking the water with her arms. She crawled a few feet toward land, turned and sat again, staring sullenly at the ocean.

Defeated, she picked up a handful of sand and threw it at the waves.

Her moment was lost.

Zachary could see Manny coming from far away, his lean figure in a yellow swimsuit. Manny took long strides in the surf. The children, carrying their spears of fish, ran alongside, trying to keep up with him. As he passed the almost-tranced Mexican woman, he nodded her way and said in his best raspy Gable, "Good afternoon, Scarlett. You don't look well."

Manny pulled a chair up next to Zachary, took Zachary's bottle and tipped it up for a deep drink.

"Back so soon?" Zachary asked, having to erase his imaginary story of Manny's long afternoon tryst with a beautiful stranger.

"You want me to go away, come back later?"

"No." Lately, Zachary had trouble distinguishing Manny's usual smart-ass remarks from genuine anger and disgust. They sat in awkward silence, Manny staring straight out to sea.

"I wonder what it's like in Portugal," Zachary said, suddenly remembering the origins of this increasingly disasterous trip and trying to initiate a pleasant conversation.

"*Uno Superior*," Manny said to a waiter. "No, make it two. *Dos*. One for my amigo here."

"You want to go to Portugal?" Zachary asked to gauge Manny's state of mind.

"Why not," Manny said, with a flicker of contempt in his voice and an unfriendly look in his green eyes. "It doesn't make any difference where you wait. Waiting is waiting."

It was a remark that may have defined Manny's situation, whatever that was, Zachary thought; but its application to Zachary didn't go unnoticed. He thought of the Mexican woman. How many moments do you get?

There was another long silence, interrupted by the return of the waiter who handed them two perspiring Superiors. Zachary fished out 400 pesos.

"I'm going for a swim," Manny said. "Care to join me?"

"No, I think I'll just . . ." Zachary realized the next words would be *wait here,* so he didn't finish the sentence.

Manny swallowed a good fourth of his beer in one gulp and was off running. Once his feet hit the surf, he leaped, his body perfectly straight, and sliced through a cresting wave.

Zachary had read through twenty pages before the sun came directly at him, making it impossible to continue. He started to look at his watch. It was gone. Had he forgotten to put it on? No. No, he hadn't. How very strange, Zachary thought.

He must have forgotten. "Oh, God," Zachary said. His sudden anxiety had nothing to do with losing something, even something that valuable. It was forgetting. Forgetting. He would trace his steps. One by one. He remembered getting up from his nap, putting on his swimming suit, putting on the short-sleeved shirt, and then, yes, putting on his watch. He could reenact it in his mind exactly. He stood up, looked in the seat of the chair, then knelt, feeling the sand. He hadn't moved from his chair. Not once.

He looked out over the beach. Only a few people were left, most of them alone, looking stranded. Perhaps he was reading too much into it. They weren't stranded, he realized. He was. He had that sinking feeling that Manny too had disappeared. He looked around for Manny. There were no heads bobbing in the ocean. Only a few sailboats, a couple of inboards, only one of which could be called a yacht. Surely, Manny wouldn't have left without saying something—even if it were something sarcastic. Nor was Manny the type to waste half a beer, Zachary thought as he looked at the perspiring, clear bottle of Superior.

Before Zachary reached the hotel room, he was already pretty sure he wouldn't find Bernard Manning there. He was right. Not only was Manny gone, so were his clothes. There wasn't so much as a note. Nothing. Zero. No evidence that he had, in fact, ever been there.

"I will not panic," Zachary told himself as the cold spray from the shower made him take a deep breath. "Life is too short to worry about things you cannot change." He said it. He didn't believe it.

Zachary searched the room for his watch, though he was convinced he would not find it. He also checked for his passport. It was there, as were all his other belongings. He went to the phone, dialed the desk clerk.

"Did Mr. Manning check out?"

"Who?"

"Mr. Manning. Bernard Manning. Manny."

"We have no Mr. Manning registered here, *señor*."

"This is Zachary Grayson. Bernard Manning and I were registered in this room, together."

"Ah, Mr. Grayson. Yes, I remember you. But I'm sorry, I do not remember your friend—a Mr. Manning, you say."

"Tall, dark, green eyes, in his early thirties?"

"I'm sorry, Mr. Grayson."

Zachary put the phone back in its cradle. This wasn't possible. Bernard Manning had signed the card. Grayson had paid for two people. He would go to the police.

Zachary slipped on his white cotton shirt, gray and white seersucker slacks, and sandals. Retrieving his wallet, keys, and a clean, white handkerchief, it suddenly struck him. He'd heard Manny on the phone and he remembered the address clearly. He remembered the Spanish because he tried to translate. Though he missed most of the conversation and couldn't speak Spanish beyond what he'd learned from reading and the movies, he knew the numbers and recognized the particular saint the street was named after.

He would go to the address first. If he could not be satisfied, then he would go to the police. He would put it in their hands and he would fly home in the morning.

11 In the Tower Foundation office located between Congress and the White House, Jeremiah Tower rarely sat at his monumental desk—and never when he had visitors. Instead, he sat with his guests in the more informal setting several feet away in one of a pair of oversized wingbacks which flanked the sofa in a separate area of the large, mahogany-paneled office. The masculine, clubby feel of the dark wood revealed an office not unlike that of his study in Georgetown, except that it was larger and had few of his personal mementos.

"Why on earth did we send Bernard Manning on this?" Tower asked. The soft and friendly tone of his voice belied both the words he spoke and the cold gray eyes peering from under bushy silver eyebrows. "I thought he was to be used as a courier."

"We thought that Manning was right because he speaks flawless Spanish. He's low profile—virtually unknown. Since Congress has us in its sights, so to speak, we thought he was best. And well, frankly, that's what we thought this was—simply a pickup."

Former aide to Indiana Senator Dawkins, Will Jessup, kept the nervousness from his voice, but his constant shifts in his chair gave him away.

"You're a bit in the hot seat, too, I understand." Tower uncrossed his legs, ready to show the younger man to the double mahogany doors. "Your name is in that new Reagan years exposé."

"I'm in no danger. Well, only if the general talks. I've been questioned, of course."

"No great loss, I suspect," Tower said.

"I'm sorry, I don't understand," Jessup said.

Tower laughed. "I didn't mean you, of course. I meant, that if we lose this little computer chip, it's not as if we've lost something we had. It merely means that we won't get something we want. Don't you think that's true?"

"Of course that's not true, Mr. Tower." Jessup was well aware of Tower's way of testing whether someone was really in the program. "I'm not sure it's lost yet."

"Yet?" Tower raised his eyebrows. Smiled.

"I know that Manning has the reputation of being a loose cannon, but he has never really failed before. This isn't nuclear fission we're talking about here."

"Isn't it?"

"I know the chip is important . . ."

"I thought you said you didn't know anything about this computer chip?" Tower said.

"What I'm trying to say is that I'm sure that whatever it is, it's important and has top priority—over everything—but that Bernard Manning's task didn't require a lot of special skills. I didn't want to use anyone higher up because I don't know how far their intelligence has penetrated."

"Does he know what this is all about?"

"No. He just knows he is supposed to pick up something from someone in Puerto Vallarta."

"Are you sure?"

"I've been giving him his orders and *I* don't know what it's about. You said computer chip, that's the first I've heard of it."

"Oh," Tower said, his left eye twitching. He got out of his chair. "Where is he now?"

"I don't know."

"And the package, the chip?" Tower had his hand on the crystal doorknob.

"We've lost track of the carrier."

"I understand your Bernard Manning took someone with him to Puerto Vallarta."

"Seems so." Jessup was tiring of the cross examination.

"Seems so? Will, this doesn't seem to be a very tightly run operation."

"No, it doesn't, sir. I don't know what to say."

"Who has it, the Mexican intermediary or Manning?"

"I don't know."

"What about them?"

"We know they've sent Earl Patrick. We received a report he was heading to Mexico. We figure it has to be for this."

"And who is he?"

"Muscle."

"What a term, Will. Muscle." Tower smiled. We've got a couple of inept carrier pigeons and they have muscle. We're supposed to have the elite squads, Will, aren't we?"

"Yes, of course." Jessup was sweating. He was praying that Tower would just open the goddamn doors and let him out.

"Why don't you use your handkerchief, Will. It's a little stuffy in here, isn't it?"

"I might be coming down with something," Jessup volunteered.

"Yes, you very well might." Tower opened one of the doors. "Warm shower, some juice, and early to bed. Right?"

"That sounds good, Mr. Tower. Thank you."

"Oh Will, you don't know the significance of the computer chip, you say?"

"No." Jessup said.

"No thoughts about it?"

Will Jessup wiped his brow. More needling, more game playing. Tower was a pompous ass.

"It strikes me that given the nature of our interests, the chip probably has a significant economic impact for our clients." Jessup failed to conceal the animosity he felt.

"Indeed," Tower said. He smiled.

Tower went to his desk, took out a single sheet of white paper and a pen. He wrote: *That stock from the local firm we discussed. Too risky. Call in the chips, then sell.*

By the time Zachary's taxi reached the address, the day was about to end. The light had turned to a soft, warm gold. He fumbled with a few Spanish phrases, trying to convince the driver to wait. But the driver had his hand out, waving it, demanding payment.

Zachary paid and the man drove off. Zachary went to the heavy wooden door, surprised to find it open. He knocked on it just the same.

"Manny," he called. "Manny, I need to talk with you, just for a few seconds."

Zachary edged inside carefully. It was dark, damp. "Anybody here?" He crept through the dusty dining room, toward a room that had a bit more light. He could see an outside garden through the dirty glass.

"Excuse me, anybody here? Manny?"

The door to the outside was open, too. He approached it. Outside, a lawn chair rested on its side. And there in the pool was a body, face down in the grimy water, the visible portions of the body barely distinguishable from the other debris.

Whoever it was had long hair. A woman, he was pretty sure. Zachary felt sick. Back on the street, moving quickly from the house, he tried to dismiss the thought that Manny was somehow connected, that it might have been Manny who killed her. After all, how much did Zachary know about the handsome stranger and his mysterious prowling? Manny, his traveling companion cum drug smuggler, was perhaps a professional hit man. Christ!

He could not call the police. Not now. What would he tell them? That while he was searching for a man whose existence he could not confirm, he walked uninvited into the house of someone he didn't know only to discover a dead body he couldn't identify? At worst, they might think he did it or was at least in on it. At best, they would merely think him insane. Either way, Zachary would no doubt be held in some horrid jail for God knows how long. All Zachary really wanted right now was to be magically transported back to his condo on Green and Greenwich, or to wake up and find this was only a nightmare.

Zachary's mind was flung into a panic a few degrees short of hysteria. He wanted out.

Perhaps it was some sort of Lutheran guilt that intervened. He was, after all, a responsible adult. There was moral action to be taken. Someone was missing, perhaps in danger. Someone was dead. Murdered. Maybe. Maybe not murdered. Perhaps the poor woman committed suicide. Maybe it was an accident. Heart attack. Hardly a heart attack. She was fully clothed, floating in a filthy swimming pool. Wouldn't family members have to be notified?

Wait, wait, wait, he told himself. This isn't San Francisco. This is Mexico. Corrupt authorities, red tape. He definitely had to get out. Where would he go now? Probably have to stay the night. If he had to, he'd rent a car and drive out of there. He tried to still his mind. No need to sort it out now. He couldn't think clearly. His mind would not stop for a single, coherent moment.

Earl Patrick knew he'd never win a beauty contest. He also knew that his barrel-chested body and his tough, angular face were enough of a threat that he could intimidate others with his presence. But there was more to his personal armory. He'd developed his voice while a drill instructor for the Marines. They taught him how to use the diaphragm to bring the sound up from deep inside in a way that scared the shit out of the recruits. Thirty years of chain-smoking cigarettes and guzzling vodka didn't hurt either. They had given Patrick's already deep voice the quality of a saw cutting through hardwood.

The Marines also taught Earl Patrick the art of destroying a person's resistance, breaking him down. That skill was refined by his current employer. And this would come in handy with young Bernard Manning. If a little psychological torture didn't work, there was always the physical version.

Those who were acquainted with Patrick would be surprised to learn he preferred the former, though the latter was quicker. He really didn't enjoy hurting people. His regular prostitute back home in Cleveland would be surprised to learn that he did, in fact, hurt people from time to time. All she knew was a quiet, gentle man, who gave her money and brought her groceries.

He wished he were in Cleveland right now, watching a baseball game and shacking up with Jennifer. But what Patrick had to find out was if Manning had made the pickup or whether the Mexican kid still had the goods. Patrick was pretty sure the contact hadn't been made. Otherwise, Manning wouldn't be hanging around, playing in the Pacific with the dolphins.

At the moment, Bernard Manning was locked inside an abandoned fuel tanker. Earl Patrick was waiting—waiting for the dark confinement to begin to loosen Bernard Manning's resolve. It would take a couple of days. It had been made clear to him by his new contact that time was considerably less important than accomplishment.

Manny was cold. One of the guys, the one who pulled him in from the water a half mile from the Mexican beach, forced him to undress before shoving him in the hole. His nakedness, the darkness and the cool ocean surrounding the metal chamber accounted for the chill. The fall was steep, maybe twelve to fourteen feet, but he hadn't broken anything. He had space to move around. There was nothing in this tank but himself.

The effect of the curved space was strange. It seemed to Manny as if the walls that confined him were endless. There was a faint, constant lapping sound and gentle, subtle shifts in the floor as the small tanker was lifted and dropped in the water by the tide.

Manny had no idea how long he'd been there. There were no reference points. Time, like space, meant little. He laid down, feeling the chill of the cool metal against his naked flesh. He curled in a fetal position, trying to heat his body with the warmth of his own body temperature, something he understood would have a constantly diminishing effect.

The reason for this kind of confinement was not lost on Manny. He knew it was intended to make him more vulnerable. The irony was, of course, that he had nothing of value to give his captors in exchange for freedom or a merciful death. He also knew his captors would not believe him. Given the nature of this business, that much was obvious.

Manny had no doubt they would kill him if it suited them. They killed the woman, didn't they? Somebody did. Before joining Zachary on the beach, Manny had visited her to see if she had any more word on the person he was to contact, and found her floating in the pool. Then, after nearly being run over by the speedboat, he was snatched from the ocean and thrown in the tank. No words. Nothing. Who were they?

The one guy could be Polish. He was big, built like a bear and had a jagged face. His friend, a slim Mexican made no sound either, simply held a knife at Manny's throat from the time he was pulled from the water until he was dropped in the tank. How many hours ago had that happened?

"Shit," Manny said. "They also have a key to the hotel room." It had fallen on the deck when the Latino cut off his Speedo, the blade coming all too close to parts of his anatomy that he was particularly fond of. They could easily trace the key back to the hotel, to the room, and to Zachary.

"That poor man," Manny said. Then it suddenly occurred to him: Maybe this was all Grayson's doing; that this quiet, docile man he'd been asked to get close to was a helluva lot more than a food writer. He wasn't using Grayson. Grayson was using him. It made sense.

12 It was the effort to escape from the dream that awakened Zachary. His eyes opened to the darkness. In the quiet, he heard breathing. It was not his own. He wasn't quite sure what caused him to notice the shadow, the dark figure standing beside the bed. Perhaps it was the moonlight or reflections through the open window from the street lamps below.

For a moment he thought he was still dreaming. Suddenly he was aware of the breathing, louder now, above the hum of the overhead fan as it made indistinct circles above the shadow's head. Zachary caught a glint of silver. It moved. He knew it was a knife. He saw its arc as the man raised the knife above his head. Knew that it would come down and plunge into him.

It was too late to move. Zachary closed his eyes, body tensed, brittle, in anticipation of the act. He could even imagine it. Sharp pain, then the warmth of the blood, then pain, and life would drift away. If he were still dreaming, he would wake up. If not, he would be dead. The only thing he could feel was indifference. Dead? Alive? No matter.

Zachary felt a crush of weight come across his chest. It was sudden. It did not feel like what he had anticipated. No pain. Instead, suffocation. His lungs would not expand. He could not breathe.

He could still think. He bit his tongue. He could still feel. He opened his eyes to see the vague whirring of the overhead fan. He felt the weight sliding off him. Then he was free of it. He heard a thump, and then a voice.

"Are you all right?" There was light. Zachary saw the boy in the red satin swimsuit. He was kneeling beside a crumpled body on the floor, pulling an ice pick from the dead man's back where it had lodged just below the neck.

Neither of them said anything for a long time. The kid just looked at Zachary, and Zachary stared blankly at the boy who had read his fortune.

"Hello," the kid said.

"What's going on?" Zachary finally asked, dazed.

"I don't know. This man wanted to kill you, I guess." The kid said it matter-of-factly.

"What are you doing here?"

"I came back to return the watch," the boy said, pulling Zachary's watch from his swimsuit. "Then I wasn't sure if I wanted to give it back. So I sit in your bathroom for a while, thinking. Nobody would give me what it's worth here. But I thought maybe I could get more in Mexico City."

Zachary shook his head, as if trying to shake whatever sense into it he needed to understand what was making absolutely no sense at all.

"Then I heard someone putting a key in your door," the kid continued. "I don't know, maybe you have a friend, I think. I don't know what to do. I waited. Then I saw the knife. He was going to kill you. That made me mad. You're a nice man. Maybe a robbery. Okay. Because you have a lot of money. But I don't know why somebody need to kill you. So I kill him."

Sali, holding the knife in one hand, rolled the body over with the other and began going through the pockets.

"If you are thinking to call the police, don't do it," Sali said firmly.

Most of the dead man's pockets were empty. Sali found only a few pesos, some matches, and a package of cigarettes.

"I hadn't thought that far ahead," Zachary said, hurrying to the bathroom.

"If you do, you will never get to leave. Americans involved in the killings of Mexicans stay a long time or pay a lot of money."

"What would they do to you?" Zachary called back from the bathroom.

"If they catch me, who knows? It would give them happiness to put me away for a while." Sali put the pesos in his makeshift swimsuit and lit a cigarette from the dead man's pack.

The face of the corpse was expressionless. He was young, maybe in his twenties. He wore sandals, baggy pants, and a white shirt, unbuttoned in the front.

"Do you know him?" Zachary asked, coming back into the room.

"You want a cigarette?" Sali offered Zachary the pack.

"No, thank you."

"I don't know him. Do you?" Sali asked.

"No."

"He wanted to kill you."

"I don't know why. There are a lot of things I don't know

right now. A friend of mine disappears. The hotel desk clerk says he doesn't exist or at least that he didn't register, though I saw him sign his name below mine. Someone he visited yesterday goes for a permanent dip in the pool. And a young boy tells me my fortune, steals my watch, then returns it in time to kill a man who is trying to murder me—all for no apparent reason. And I've been here not quite two days." Zachary shook his head. "In this small, quiet, sunny resort in Mexico."

"This person isn't from Puerto Vallarta. And I think he was paid to kill you."

"Why is that?"

"He carries nothing to tell who he is. Not even a picture of his mother."

"Maybe. How do you know he isn't from here?"

"Because this is a small place."

"I think we have to tell the police," Zachary said. "It's getting too complicated. I should have done it earlier."

"You, only maybe. Me . . ." He brought the knife across his throat. *"Pffft."*

"Then what do we do? Leave him for the maid?"

Sali, who was still kneeling, started laughing. He rocked back on his haunches, tears coming from his eyes, arms holding his stomach. "Yes, mister," he said, trying to catch his breath. "You are very funny. I like you."

Sali went to the phone, picked up the receiver and handed it to Zachary. "Ask the desk clerk to give you 53472."

"Who's that?" Zachary looked puzzled.

"Give me the phone when you hear it ringing."

Zachary obeyed.

Sali spoke for only a moment, a total of five words maybe, none of which Zachary understood. Then the young Mexican hung up, went to the chair by the window and sat.

"What was that all about?" Zachary asked.

"Wait," Sali said. He went to the window and stared into the abandoned streets. "You can hear the ocean from here. I can hear it too, from where I live. It's very nice."

Manny was cold to the bone. It wasn't that snowy, icy cold that invited you to lay down and go to sleep. It was merely an irritating cold. He couldn't escape it. Whether he sat or stretched out prone, his naked flesh pressed against the cool metal. Best to let only the bottom of his feet touch; but he could not stand or walk forever. He tried pacing off the dimensions but could not determine just how large a cell it was because there were no corners, no straight lines. He had jumped a few times but could not touch the top. He had run his fingers across the cold surface, every inch of it, he thought, and found nothing—only a few small holes with jagged edges, which he imagined were once connections for a ladder.

Finally he sat down and felt the cold surface against the cheeks of his ass. There was a sound of metal on metal, surfaces grating against one another. Then there was a tiny half moon of light from above.

"How are you doing, young man?" said Earl Patrick, peering down into the darkness.

"Well, you see, there's a problem."

"I'm sure there is."

"I have to take a piss."

"That's no problem. You'll never fill the place up."

"Also, I appreciate the guest room, but I've misplaced my wallet. And I don't know the American Express phone number."

Suddenly there was a light in Manny's eyes. It was a broad shaft of light that illuminated his naked body. He felt small and frail in the darkness, but even more so in the light. He shivered. His knees knocked against one another. He felt ashamed and angry, but he refused to let it show.

"My laundry isn't back yet. You mind?" There was a long silence. "You like looking at naked guys?"

The light went off.

"Bernard Manning. . . ." said the voice.

"That's what my mommy named me."

"Under the conditions, Bernie, your mama would want you to cooperate. She'd want you to tell us where to find this little computer chip."

"I always do what my mommy says, mister, but I don't know what the fuck you're talking about."

He heard the grating sound and watched as the little, half moon of light disappeared.

In five minutes the phone rang. Sali got it. At first the conversation was congenial, but Sali's voice got louder, angrier. Zachary reminded him of the hour and Sali went into an intense whisper.

When he hung up, Sali told Zachary to stay there. He would wait down on the street. In minutes, Sali said, the body would be gone.

Zachary stared at the body. The eyes were still open, glazed over, much like the eyes of the fish he saw on the beach. It took him several minutes to work up the courage to reach down and close the dead eyes.

He went to the window, looked down to see if the boy was indeed waiting below. He could not see him. Perhaps he was in the doorway. Then again, more likely, the boy had left—left Zachary in the hotel room with a body and a flimsy story about some kid who happened to pop in just in time to slay a would-be murderer. "What kid?" they would ask. And what could he tell them? He didn't even know the kid's name. "A fortune teller," he would say. Right.

What a fool he was. The boy was gone. Was there any doubt? Zachary remembered the movie *Midnight Express* and imagined himself in a Mexican prison, crawling on dirt floors, searching for scraps of food. Then he laughed. *Nouvelle Prison Cuisine: 101 Ways to Prepare a Cockroach.*

The laugh diminished to a smile and the smile gave way to reality. He must do something. What should he do? He walked to the window and back several times, hoping to catch a glimpse of the boy. How silly it was for a man near middle age to wait to be rescued by a teenage boy.

A truck drove up, a battered old pickup. Two men got out and Zachary saw the boy go meet them. They talked, but in such low tones that Zachary couldn't hear what was said. He could only make out their emotions by the rapid movement of their hands.

They followed the boy, disappearing underneath the building. Soon they reappeared in Zachary's doorway. The chubby one carried a burlap bag, the kind used for a hundred-pound potato sack.

"What are you doing with those?" Zachary asked.

"For the body," Sali said.

The chubby Mexican reached into the bag and pulled out another one just like it. The other pulled out a small hacksaw and a butcher knife.

"Two bags. One body," Zachary said. He swallowed audibly and went to the window for air. "No," he said.

"No?" Sali asked.

"No." Zachary shook his head and kept shaking it. He

wasn't about to add dismemberment to the long list of horrors he'd experienced so far.

"How do we get the body out?" Sali's eyes widened. "Okay. We will walk the body."

Sali spoke to his sidekicks. They were to pretend the dead man was drunk. They were helping him home.

Zachary could hear them singing below the window. A door shut, then another. He heard the truck pull away.

Sali stayed behind.

13 Will Jessup's life was blessed. After serving with Senator Dawkins, he was hired by Jeremiah Tower, director of a Washington, D.C., think tank at a very handsome salary. Tower helped Jessup find this wonderful place in Georgetown, just far enough off the main street to feel tucked away with the best of Washington society.

Jessup's connections with the Senator and with the secret government made him invaluable to the insiders who make a lot of things happen. With the last elections, the Iran-Contra flap had blown over for good. There was the little matter of the general; but there were bigger buns than his ready to fry first. And if somebody did want to make something of it, he had enough on enough people to keep himself out of it. He even had some things on Tower, about whom he wasn't feeling too kindly at the moment. What did Tower expect, anyway? It wasn't Jessup's fault the carrier didn't find Manny.

Jessup was thirty-five, handsome, fit, and, aside from a

slightly messy divorce, had a pretty good rep. He'd done enough favors to make a political move of his own someday.

He kept a home in Indianapolis—an apartment really—for residence requirements, had an in with that city's most prestigious law firm and fully expected to be Senator Jessup in less than five years. At worst, he might have to run for governor or accept an appointment in Washington. He would marry again in a few years. In the meantime, there was ravishing Rebecca Townsend, a secretary at the Office of the Interior.

Will Jessup brushed his teeth, gave a toothy grin to the mirror, and took a gulp of blue-green liquid. He let it swirl around in his mouth and spit it out. "A mere secretary," he said to himself in the mirror. "And a voluptuous vixen. And she said she'd be right over."

Before he turned the light off on the table next to his bed, he pulled a contraceptive from the drawer. He tore it open so he wouldn't have to fumble in the dark. He turned off the light. If he went to sleep, Rebecca had a fantastic way of waking him up.

He could feel himself drifting off into sleep. He fought it by thinking about Jeremiah Tower. Just as Jessup was leaving, Tower had called him back in. They exchanged a few words. Tower had been vaguely threatening. Perhaps, Jessup shouldn't have done it, but he put Tower in his place with a few vague threats of his own.

Will Jessup heard sounds in the darkness. He smiled. He would pretend to be asleep. He was getting an erection just thinking about her.

There was a hand over his mouth. But it wasn't a woman's. It was rough and smelled of nicotine. There was a hand on his chest. He opened his eyes but saw nothing. Someone was pulling the blankets off of him. The beam from the flashlight moved down his body quickly. Jessup saw a hypodermic. Someone laughed.

A voice said: "He was ready for something, but not this."

Jessup felt someone grab his feet, spread his toes. He felt the pinprick. It didn't hurt. What was going on? Was he being kidnapped? Hands held him. Then, suddenly and with great force, he felt as if someone had just punched him in the heart. Jessup's brain filled with clouds. The pain was gone.

Manny's dilemma was that he would never know whether he had enough toughness to keep from spilling his guts to his captors, because he had nothing to spill. Questions concerning his strength of character could not be answered. Morality wasn't in question either, though mortality certainly was.

If there were such things as good and evil—and he'd pretty much dismissed that idea years ago—Manny had no idea whether he was working for the good guys or the bad guys. Was the overweight Cuban in Miami a good guy? What about the woman cashier at the porno palace?

Bernard Manning was, in fact, in the dark—in more ways than merely being in the cold, dank belly of a tanker.

Manny heard the grating sound. It could only have been a few minutes since the last time, unless time itself was really getting out of hand. There was no light at first.

"Bernie?" came Earl Patrick's voice. It was warm, friendly.

"My friends call me Manny."

"Manny, it's going to be a while until we talk again. I thought you might want to tell me a few things so I could let you go."

"I've got this problem, you see. And it's that somebody, I don't know who, tells me to go to Mexico. They tell me someone will give me something. I suppose when I bring it back they will tell me who to give it to. That's it."

"Who's your contact, Manny?"

"I don't know."

"Who's the fag you're traveling with?"

"Cover. Protection. He's not involved. If he is, he's on your side. Whose side is that anyway?"

"Cover? Protection from who?"

"Whom?" Silence. "You, apparently," Manny answered, deciding the guy was as much into grammar as he was humor. "Listen, I've got a question. I mean, I've been thinking down here a lot. What I want to know is: Are you a good guy or a bad guy?"

"Sarcasm? C'mon, Manny. Between friends?" A light shown from the top—a shaft of light coming straight down into the darkness making a sharp circle on the metal floor.

"Come on over here, Manny, stand in the light."

"Why?"

"Because I want you to. I'm not going to shoot you. If I wanted to do that I could shoot you at will. There's no place to hide. You're a monkey in a barrel down there."

"I don't want to. I mean you haven't been very nice to me, have you? I tell you my name, what my friends call me. I answer your questions and you won't tell me whether you're a good guy or a bad guy."

"It's about your attitude, Manny. Did anyone ever tell you you're insincere? Now, how can I take your answers about not knowing anything when you kid around like that? You know what I mean? I'm doing my job and you're being a smart-ass."

"You'll like me a lot better when you get to know me." Something fell into the circle of light. A blanket. Manny went over, leaned down to pick it up. Suddenly his body was drenched with water with such force that it knocked him down.

"Yeah Manny, we'll both sit around, have a few beers, and have a good laugh about this someday, won't we?" The light went out.

Zachary slumped down on the edge of the bed, head in hands.

"Why would anyone want to kill me?"

"Did you do something bad to someone?" Sali asked, sitting down beside him.

"I can't imagine arousing that kind of passion in anyone. No. No one I can think of . . ."

"Don't forget your watch." Sali gestured toward the bedside table.

"I won't. Thank you. What made you bring it back? Never mind. Can I help you in some way. Do you need money?"

"I need a bath. Where I am staying, there isn't any."

"Sure. Help yourself. But I think we should leave soon. They—whoever *they* are—might be back."

Sali walked across the room to the bathroom, turned on the water, and took off his red satin swimsuit.

"It might look funny," Sali said, picking up the pesos that had fallen to the floor, "if you check out in the middle of the night. Besides, I asked my friends to watch. They owe me favors. Leave in the morning."

He wrapped a towel around his slender waist and went to the window.

Such smooth brown skin, Zachary thought. Beautiful.

"How old are you?"

"Eighteen," Sali said.

"You don't look eighteen."

"I'm small. My parents were small, I think. Is it important how old I am?"

"I don't know. You just seem wise beyond your years."

"Where will you go?" Sali asked, leaning out of the window to look both ways down the promenade.

"Home."

"Where do you live?"

"San Francisco."

Sali nodded. "How will you get there?" He sat in the chair across from Zachary. He began rubbing his toes and the nakedness beneath the towel drew Zachary's eyes in.

"Fly." Zachary turned his head away.

"From Mazatlán?" Sali asked.

"I don't know. I don't care. I just want out of here."

"There's a bus that leaves for Mazatlán tomorrow morning."

"No buses," Zachary said. "I'll rent a car or something. Who knows, maybe I'll drive to Mexico City—whatever it takes . . ."

"Quicker to Mazatlán. Even that is a thousand kilometers."

Zachary tried to convert kilometers to miles, but gave up in disgust. "In the morning," he said. "I'll think about it in the morning."

"Okay," Sali said, heading for the bathroom.

Zachary's eyes followed involuntarily.

"You like me?" Sali asked, undoing his towel, holding one end of it and allowing the other to fall to the floor.

Zachary couldn't answer.

"It's all right if you do," Sali said matter-of-factly.

"The water's running," Zachary said.

The boy leaned against the door frame. "It makes me feel good for someone to look at me. To like me." Sali's body was silhouetted by the bathroom light behind him. "Your eyes tell me . . ."

Zachary interrupted. "My God, I'm three times your age." He regretted his harsh, judgmental tone immediately. He felt not only old, but foolish.

"Yes," the boy said with a grin. "You don't want to take advantage of someone who knows so little about life."

Sali turned, went into the bathroom, gently shutting the door behind him.

Jeremiah Tower took a sip of orange juice as his maid brought a soft-boiled egg and toast without butter. He unfolded the newspaper. He leafed through until he found a relatively small story buried deep in the paper.

FORMER AIDE DIES OF HEART ATTACK

The body of William P. Jessup, 35, a former assistant to Indiana Senator Harold Dawkins, was found late last night by a member of his staff.

"Will often worked late," said Rebecca Townsend, Jessup's administrative assistant at Tower Enterprises, a Washington, D.C.–based conservative think tank. "I had just talked to him on the phone," she said, "and agreed to help him compile a report for a meeting tomorrow morning."

Jessup, who had a history of heart problems, was considered a rising star on the Washington political scene. Once associated with the Iran-Contra affair, the recently divorced Jessup was regarded by many as charismatic and a potential candidate for high public office.

"I could tell he wasn't feeling well," said Jeremiah

Tower, the influential 65-year-old head of the foundation
that bears his name. "When we talked yesterday afternoon,
Will said he thought he was coming down with a cold."

Services for Jessup, dead of an apparent heart attack at
mid-career, are expected to be held in Indianapolis and
Washington, D.C.

"He was dedicated, hardworking, and a real patriot,"
Tower said. "We're going to miss him. So will the country."

Tower wished the paper hadn't mentioned the Iran-Contra
connection, but for the most part, it was a pretty safe story.
After all, he thought, the dealings Jessup had had with that
sticky situation would be buried with him. Tower smashed the
side of the egg with his spoon, watching the contents spill out
over the jagged edge of the broken shell.

14 It was quiet when Zachary awoke. He went to the window. The sun was out. But the usual bustle on the streets was absent. He remembered only a snatch of his dream—Sali on the beach in his red swimsuit, unconscious, the tide pulling him out to sea.

Moments passed before Zachary remembered the events of the night. It was a jolt. Perhaps it was just one more dream. He looked around the room for signs. There were none. No blood. He tried to remember if there had been blood somewhere. He couldn't be sure.

He noticed the towel hanging on the open bathroom door. It was Sali's. The watch? It was on the bedside table, where the boy had put it. Zachary started to pick it up when he noticed his diary laying open—an ashtray at its center to keep the pages from flipping.

There was a message. He put on his glasses and saw handwriting. Not his own, but easily decipherable.

You said you would help me. Maybe I can ride with you to Mazatlán. I need to leave very soon, too. I will come by at 8 o'clock. Please wait for me. P.S. Who is Manny?

"The little devil read my diary," Zachary said, not concerned about talking to himself. He looked at the watch—eight forty-five. He pulled at his glasses. "He's already late!"

Zachary shoved his clothes into his one large suitcase, periodically looking out of the window for some sign of the boy.

"Come on, Sali," Zachary heard himself say. "I haven't got all day."

Zachary waited for the boy until he could no longer believe the boy was coming. He waited three hours. He was angry. Angry at Sali because he was a liar. Because he was a thief. Because he was unreliable. Because he was nosy. Because he had cared enough about him to wait three goddamn hours.

No matter how hard Manny tried, there was no way to get warm. The blanket was wet. He was wet. Even his goose pimples had goose pimples. It was simple. If he did not get out of there, he would die—either at the hands of his captors or from pneumonia.

Manny had completely lost track of time. He had no idea whether hours, minutes, or days had passed since his captor doused him with a bucket of salt water. Without food, drink, light, warmth, and with only the strange lapping sound and an occasional metal clang echoing in his hollow chamber, Manny was in a physical if not yet mental void.

He thought maybe he had actually slept awhile, rather than having dozed off. He wasn't sure. He thought he saw a shadow even darker than the pitch darkness he was in and moved around the seemingly endless space in search of it. The only things his fingers felt were the metal lining of his cell and himself.

Manny had been hungry. No more. The feeling wore off. Thirst hadn't worn off. He was still thirsty. The puddle of water on the floor was salt water. It was still there as was the soggy blanket.

The desk clerk did all the official stamping and signing to un-register his guest. When Zachary asked to see the registration he and Manny had signed when they registered days ago, the clerk smiled and told him someone had spilled wine on it. And they had to make up a duplicate.

For Zachary this was a relief. He had begun to doubt his sanity, wondering if it might not be possible to have imagined Manny in the first place. This little subterfuge on the part of the clerk was reassuring.

The clerk did tell Zachary where he might find a car to rent and was kind enough to provide him with a frayed road map of central Mexico. Perhaps this was a sign things were improving.

Zachary tipped him a thousand pesos. Maybe the planets realigned more favorably. Maybe his biorythyms had stabilized or yin and yang had suddenly balanced. Perhaps he was up to date with the payments on his karmic debt. Whatever it was, it was about time, he thought.

If someone had told Zachary he'd be driving halfway across Mexico—alone—he would have laughed. Europe, maybe. He checked his wallet. Had he thought to bring his driver's license? Was it up to date? He didn't own a car. Hadn't for twenty years. The last time he drove was in France, two years ago. A Peugeot, a black, shiny Peugeot, gliding through the civilized French countryside—fine wine, fine food, and no attempts to send him into the hereafter. Yes, he had his license. It was good for another eight months.

"American Chef Slain on Mexican Highway." Zachary could see the headlines. "Famous American Gourmet Arrested for Murder." He would be arrested for some minor infraction of the law. The police would link him with the killing of the woman or the man, and Zachary would rot in a Mexican jail along with American kids arrested for smoking marijuana. He'd read about that in the *Chronicle* years ago.

He shifted his suitcase to his left side. Beads of perspiration formed over his brow. He hoped the car had air-conditioning.

He imagined a posthumous book on the presses. It would stun his friends. His bland life would suddenly have the makings of a biography, a lurid unauthorized—of course, unauthorized—biography hinting at espionage, murder, and lurid affairs with young boys. That would be one way to get the spotlight from Craig Claiborne.

Standing on the street corner, waiting for a small parade of automobiles to pass, Earl Patrick was impatient. Things weren't going particularly well. His partner, sent to the food writer's hotel, had failed to return. Manny wasn't talking. And a coded phone call from Washington told him that the computer chip was still out there somewhere, and for him to get it.

Still, there was a bright side. Once done, Earl Patrick could go back to Cleveland. Except for the faggot, Patrick at least knew the players. Then it dawned on him—perhaps Manny was the decoy and the fag was the real courier. Certainly the failure of his partner to return meant something.

He had the little Mexican kid—the small hand bloodless in Patrick's ham-fisted grip. Benito, another Mexican, less reliable than Patrick's lost partner, stood on the other side of Sali. Benito had a switchblade tucked in the waistband of the boy's makeshift swimsuit. There was another American, called in from Mexico City, walking behind them.

"You know what happens, kid, when your spinal column is cut?" Patrick asked, guiding the youth through the streets just now filling with people heading to church. "You get to live, but you ain't happy about it." It was a long walk to the car. They would have to go all the way back through town.

Manny remembered how prisoners of war kept their sanity by playing games of chess or by building houses, brick by brick. However, Manny didn't know how to play chess and had very little interest in building houses. After searching his mind for the things that he loved, he could only come up with alcohol and women—neither of which seemed particularly constructive for maintaining an alert mind, merely reminders of an existence given to states of drugged repression and instant gratification.

Language had been his love once. He remembered going to school with a bunch of Italian kids. It was in elementary school, maybe third grade, when he discovered that several of these kids could speak English in class, but often spoke Italian among their friends. In Manny's mind, these kids had a sort of special bond, a secret society separate from the rest, from the teachers and from the other classmates.

Manny, a skinny kid with a big nose, lousy in sports, was also separate from the rest. He had no friends. His father, who worked two jobs, spent the rest of his time in an alcoholic stupor. Manny suspected he inherited from his father that special gene that made him like alcohol especially well. His mom went from one nervous breakdown to the next. By the time the two of them worked their way out it and into a companionable, boring retirement, Manny was long gone. In the interim, however, he began to study Italian, then later Spanish, and French.

The Italian didn't provide entry into the world of that secret society. The Italian kids liked Manny no more than the rest of them, but Manny found he had a facility with language. That brought him some measure of respect at least among the language teachers and may have kept him from going loony, becoming another Son of Sam or someone who spent the rest of his life in a little room looking at TV through a Thorazine haze.

Then again, where was he now? His knowledge of Italian and Spanish wouldn't get him out this little blind-sided aquarium, would it? Something else: where did he get off jumping on Zachary Grayson for his passive existence? Manny's three decades plus of life on this planet weren't exactly a model of human interaction. He wasn't confronting life either. Bagging a few babes and drinking oneself into oblivion, on the whole, wasn't any better than Zachary stealing away between the covers of books and writing about the fine art of dining.

He and Zachary had more in common than he thought.

Manny took another tour of the metal chamber. At least he was thinking, moving. It wasn't completely hopeless.

The rent-a-car agency was closed. The sign dangled from the door. Church bells rang. "They toll for thee," Zachary said out loud. It was Sunday. That's why everything was so quiet.

Two battered and dusty cars remained in the lot. A single gas pump. Zachary walked to the large plate-glass window and saw himself—a perspiring, middle-aged man in rumpled clothing.

The bright sun and blue sky were behind him and his image looked like one of those hyper-real paintings of the seventies. A painfully accurate reflection.

He cupped his hands to see inside. Two empty desks. Keys with cardboard tags hung on nails in the wall. A filing cabinet, with more paper stacked on it than would fit into it, but no sign of life.

Zachary started back toward town, regretting his generosity to the desk clerk. The guy had to know it was Sunday. Maybe it was a plot to get Zachary out into a desolate part of town. He looked around, hoping he wouldn't find a dark shadow lurking among the bleached buildings.

Why on earth wasn't he in San Francisco where he belonged? Why wasn't he sitting in his little office with a cup of coffee and the pink section of the *Chronicle?*

There were no clouds. The heat seemed to increase by the second. The weight of the suitcase bore into his fingers. They were going numb. He decided to leave it. What did he need from it?

He hadn't moved more than ten paces from the suitcase when he stopped.

He needed some things, didn't he? He would never find his brand of after-shave. He'd paid $125 for the razor, a self-indulgent purchase, he admitted, but important. It certainly seemed necessary at the time. And he liked his own brand of toothpaste and deodorant. Who could tell how long it would be before he got back home?

Zachary retreated to his suitcase. It stood absurdly alone in the De Chirico landscape. It had been with him for twenty years. Two weeks in Rome. A month in Japan, where Zachary had his first and only ride on the bullet train. The suitcase had gone with him to Moscow, where he was never warm; and to

Fire Island, where he was never cool and where he spent a frustrating two weeks in melancholy as he observed a gum-chewing, blond-headed youth in what amounted to a cheap beach-blanket remake of *Death in Venice*. And on to Saint Croix. Spain. Marrakech.

Then there was the pale, blue-green cashmere sweater he had searched years to find. And the worn-in pair of walking shoes that, if he had any sense, he'd be wearing now.

He picked up his suitcase, struggled with it to the rent-a-car agency, placed it in the shade of the building's overhang and sat on it, resting a bit before traipsing back into the village.

Perhaps he could grab a taxi to one of the large, luxury hotels farther down the beach, where he could rest the night and rent a decent car in the morning. He should have stayed in one of those hotels in the first place—instead of buying Manny's plea for a little local color. Local color, all right. Thieves. Dead bodies. Desertion.

Why was he carrying this ludicrous suitcase? Cheap sentiment. Stinginess. Greed. All of it could be replaced. Sweat slivered down his brows, down the lids, and into his eyes. The salt burned. The top of his head burned. He pulled out a jacket and his diary—neither of them necessities. But the nights could get cold. The jacket might come in handy. And the diary, of course, was his friend.

The diary fell open at the last entry. Zachary caught the last few words before he closed it. *Please wait for me.*

"He meant it," Zachary said, feeling he had betrayed the boy. "What do you want me to do, Sali? People just seem to disappear on me."

Zachary reconstructed the scene with the fat lady on the beach, who tried desperately to disappear but couldn't and then the lady in the swimming pool who may have wanted to stay around for a while and couldn't.

"When I die," he thought, "I want to be sitting in a comfortable beach chair, watching a beautiful, vital youth play in the surf. My own death." He laughed and thought about *Death in Venice* again. There'd be Tadzio on a skateboard. Why not? They could call it *Death in Venice Beach*.

"Your life line is split," Sali had said. "An important change."

He looked up into the sun and saw a huge black bird sitting on top of a telephone pole. It looked more like a vulture than a crow. Not much of a relief.

"*Buenos días, señor,*" said a little man who had more mustache than face. "Chew wanna renna car?"

"Yes. I mean, *sí.* I do."

Sali could feel the blade pressed against him, slightly above his buttocks. As he eyed the crowd, Earl Patrick's grip tightened. The three of them stood on the sidewalk as a policeman, obviously in his dress uniform, looked at them curiously. Behind the policeman was a slow-moving parade of automobiles. A chubby man in a white suit sat in the back of a ten-year-old Cadillac convertible.

"Must be the governor coming to town for church," Benito told Patrick.

"Fuck the goddamn governor," Patrick said through a phony, toothy smile. "He's going five fucking miles an hour. We'll wait here," Patrick looked back at the American, then fished for his keys. He tossed them to the American. "See if you can get through this mess. Get the car and come pick us up."

* * *

The man told Zachary all the best cars were out. Only two cars left. A gray 1981 Ford Fairmont that wouldn't start and a tan 1976 Pinto that would. The Pinto had air-conditioning, a straight stick, and, much to the pride of the man who opened the hood and pointed inside, a German engine.

"Theez leele babee goes!" he said. "Where chew go?"

Zachary didn't know. "Just for a drive—for a week, perhaps. I'm not quite sure, exactly."

After negotiations worthy of a nation's surrender, Zachary ended up buying it. The man, relieved to get a good price for a car with several dents, a missing bumper, bald tires, and an odometer that had to have turned over once and now rested on 12,235 miles, made relinquishing the keys a major ceremony.

Zachary reacquainted himself with the idea of operating a gear shift and clutch. He didn't venture far from the agency at first, for fear the engine would clink down on the cobblestones. But the car was surprisingly responsive. Zachary drove back through the village to get a few groceries—bottled water, if nothing else—for the trip.

Manny was tired of walking. He was tired of thinking. He slumped down, his back against the curving wall. It was a strange feeling Manny felt now—all hollow inside. It was almost as if he didn't have a body—just a thin, fragile shell. What he saw was stranger still. A still night. Cloudless. Stars. Endless.

He didn't exactly hear the laughter as much as he felt it. It was coming from out there. His body wasn't cold any longer. He really couldn't tell now where his flesh touched anything. It was as if he were floating. It was all right. Everything was all right.

15 It was the red swimsuit that caught Zachary's attention. He had no doubt it was Sali standing on the street corner, there in the crowd, attached to a rough-looking American or European. Another guy, a Mexican, looked like he was attending to the boy as well. Zachary thought the Latino looked too close, too intent upon the boy to be just another native caught in a human traffic jam. And the big guy sure as hell didn't look like a tourist.

As Zachary passed by slowly, glancing ahead to make sure he didn't overtake the tail end of what must have been a parade, Sali saw him. When Zachary turned to look at him, the boy shook his head "no" discreetly.

Zachary was surprised to find his stomach up somewhere near his throat.

He didn't stop. Instead he drove around the block and pulled to the side of the street some fifty yards away. The man or men who held Sali stood near the street, the crowd flowing around them as a river flows around a rock. Now Zachary could be sure there were two and by the anxious look on Sali's face, he wasn't in the company of friends.

The people accompanying Sali looked around them impatiently. They seemed to be waiting for someone or something. Perhaps a car. Zachary looked at them carefully. Because of his vantage point, to the flank now, he saw things he hadn't seen before. One was a bullish-looking man with very short hair, a raincoat over his arm. He stood slightly to the front of Sali. The other, standing slightly to the rear of Sali, had what appeared to be a knife and what was definitely a handful of red swimsuit.

Sali had been apprehended. But by whom? The police? Not likely. The short-haired man was not Mexican. If they were police, they weren't the local variety.

In an odd way, Zachary was relieved; there was a reason why Sali had missed his appointment this morning. This could be what Sali meant by having to leave, too. There was more to all of this than Zachary could dare conceive. But it didn't matter anyway. He had only one thing on his mind.

Zachary reached across the passenger seat, opened the car door. He reached in the backseat, retrieving his jacket, and placed it in the doorjamb so the door wouldn't close completely.

Zachary sat straight in the driver's seat and took a deep breath. He slid the gearshift into first. He wanted to be at thirty miles per hour when he got to them. Now the car was moving. He pulled the shift into second. The engine purred.

"Good old German engine. Don't move, fellas. Don't move."

Just before he got to them, one foot went to the clutch and the other crashed onto the brake pedal.

Zachary never had a clearer moment. The screech of the brakes, the passenger door flying open, smashing against the big white man, Sali getting out of the way, as the door smashed against the Mexican, lifting him up three or four feet. Zachary even caught the expressions on their faces. Confusion, anger, pain.

"Get in," Zachary said in such a commanding voice that he couldn't be sure it was his.

Sali was free, was inside the car. The force of the acceleration flung Sali backward against the seat.

"*Jesús Cristo!*" Sali said between his teeth. His eyes remained closed as Zachary flew through the gears.

"Get me out of this place," Zachary screamed.

Sali laughed.

"Directions! Directions!" Zachary yelled. "I don't know where in the hell I'm going!"

"Or what you're doing. Who are you?"

"What do you mean, who am I?"

"Like, man, who do you work for?" Sali was still smiling.

"No one. I'm a cook and a writer."

"Cooks don't do what you just did. Who are you with?"

"Simon and Schuster. Can we have our little literary chitchat later? Just concentrate on getting us someplace where there is an airplane that goes somewhere other than Mexico."

"I doubt if we will make it. A car was coming for us when you came along. They will be on us before you know it."

"Then you better keep me from going up any dead-end streets."

"You can't outrun them in this piece of shit."

"This is a fine piece of shit," Zachary said, feeling foolish about such a sudden and absurd loyalty to an automobile. "It just saved your life."

"Or maybe gets us both killed."

Palm trees flew by as the beach road began to narrow into the countryside.

"Let's not think about that."

"Right," the boy said. Zachary continued straight ahead. "Turn right!"

"Oh," Zachary said sheepishly. He nearly threw Sali into the window as he crushed the brake pedal.

"Put your seat belt on," Zachary told Sali.

The tan Pinto moved quickly into reverse. Zachary made the turn and was up to ninety miles an hour on the dirt road, when he began to slow down.

"What are you doing?" Sali asked, half-crazed.

"See that building?"

"You mean that chicken coop?"

"Yes. That's where we're going."

Zachary pulled off the road carefully, driving up the small incline, over coarse tufts of grass and small rocks, finally pulling to the rear of the dilapidated structure. He nudged the backside of the building with the nose of the car, hoping the remainder of the building held.

"No chickens," Sali said.

"Two, I think." Zachary got out of the car to look through the slats of the building. The road was fifty feet down and away from them. Zachary crouched for the vigil. Sali crouched beside him, a hand on Zachary's thighs for stability. Zachary turned.

"You mind?" Sali smiled. "I don't want to fall down."

"No." Zachary could feel the heat of each finger.

The height of the incline and the flatness of the rest of the country provided an enormous view.

Within minutes a dark car appeared on the horizon to the left. He watched it move toward them. Neither he nor Sali spoke. They barely breathed. As the car passed, Zachary could see at least three people in a large, black Chevrolet Caprice. It left a trail of swirling dust.

Far to the right, Zachary could see another dust trail. A car had pulled onto the road.

"What luck," Zachary said, laying his palm on Sali's hand.

"What?"

"A decoy. Providence has provided us with a decoy."

Sali sat back on the ground, sitting cross-legged, looking out between the wooden planks at the two swirls of dust, the second rapidly gaining on the first.

Zachary stood up, his knee cracking like dry twigs.

"That was something," Sali said.

"When you get old and lethargic, the same thing will happen to you."

"No. I mean what you did, smashing those guys."

"Yes, it was. Quite something." The adrenaline slipped away, leaving Zachary weak. He sat against the hood of the car.

"Are you okay?"

"Yes, yes, yes," Zachary said with disgust.

The trails of dust merged for a moment. The cloud dissipated. Then suddenly, the two automobiles soared off in opposite directions. The pursuers were coming back the way they'd come.

Sali held his breath.

Zachary closed his eyes. He didn't care what happened next. He was tired. Hungry. He would trade his life for a steamed lobster and a glass of anything, even a bottle of Superior.

Would they notice the turn-off marks and trace them to the shack? Was there a chance they could outrun them? Zachary got in the car, sweaty fingers on the ignition key, his eyes on the excited youth who peered out through the gap in the wall.

Suddenly Sali turned, fist clenched and with a wide, toothy grin. Zachary smiled not at the reprieve, but at the boy. His joy, his energy was, at least at the moment, contagious.

Sali slid into the passenger seat and gave Zachary a kiss on the cheek. "We can go now?"

"In a few minutes. We want to make sure they don't get a rearview mirror glimpse."

"How did you know this? I mean to hide, let them go by."

"Hopalong Cassidy."

"What?"

"Not what. Who," Zachary said.

"He did this?"

"Often. A helluva guy, that Hoppy."

"Hoppy, huh? I'm hoppy, very hoppy!" Sali laughed.

Sali guided Zachary through the back roads, from one circuitous route to another, until they reached Highway 80 to Guadalajara. En route, Sali convinced Zachary to drive all the way to Mexico City. There were people, he said, who could put him up in Cuernavaca. And Zachary could find a direct flight to San Francisco more easily in Mexico City.

For a moment, Zachary considered checking out the American Embassy in Mexico City. He could let them know that Bernard Manning might have been kidnapped. He reconsidered immediately. While he was still feeling guilty about leaving Manny to whatever fate was in store for him in Mexico, Zachary believed it would be better for all concerned if he was actually in the States when he made his bizarre claims.

The trip to the capital was 350 miles, however, not the 200 Sali implied. Halfway, Sali turned quiet. Morose.

Zachary drove through the night. Slowly. Occasionally at full stop, while Sali prodded cows off the roadway. Animals with bright red eyes stared back into the headlights. The Pinto moved over the rough roads uneasily. The engine was fine, but the body was in doubt.

Estranged from his young friend, the older man seemed to be more alone than if he rode by himself. Zachary saw only what his headlights permitted him to see and his mind was filled with questions. What was Sali running from? What was he involved with? What was Manny involved in and were the two somehow connected?

Zachary remembered what Sali had written in the diary. "Who's Manny?" Perhaps not. He would ask the boy later. There was another question that plagued Zachary Grayson. What was it that *he* and Sali had in common? An odd pair, he thought. Did he desire Sali? Yes. Would he do anything about it? No. Absolutely not.

Zachary could see his own body, milky white flesh—all of it in the process of decay, the loose skin at the neck, the thinning hair. Next to Sali's, it would seem obscene.

A trip that would normally take five hours had already grown to ten and they were still far away.

Finally in Querétaro, Zachary pulled up next to a church, shut off the lights, then the engine. He told Sali to move to the backseat. Zachary retrieved his robe from the suitcase and handed it to Sali.

"Here's your blanket."

"Why are we stopping?"

"Gas."

"Are we out?"

"Nearly. We'll stay here until morning, get some gasoline, and move on. Besides, we need the sleep."

* * *

The few hours remaining until dawn seemed eternal to Zachary. His light sleep was interrupted by Sali's moaning intercourse with his dreams. Once, the boy seemed so much in mental anguish, Zachary jostled the boy awake. Sali sat up fiercely, remained frozen for a few moments, then fell back slowly, finally placing where he was in this world.

Sali didn't speak. Eventually he drifted back into sleep, as did Zachary. The boy was quiet in the morning as well. After getting several one-word answers accompanied by a sullen glare, Zachary stopped trying to humor the boy.

They arrived in Mexico City on a steamy afternoon. They found a hotel room a few blocks off the city's celebrated thoroughfare. The clerk eyed the strange pair—one wearing a red swimsuit—with a mixture of curiosity, superiority, and contempt.

A generous tip, however, changed all that and produced a room where, a moment before, there were no vacancies. The hotel was named the Irys Astoria. Zachary was sure Irys had no relatives named Waldorf.

Zachary dialed his home phone number in San Francisco, hoping but not expecting to find Manny. No answer. He called Leslie, wanting to know if he had heard from Zachary's green-eyed companion.

"Heavens, no," Leslie said. "Have you misplaced him? You're always losing things. Where are you staying, dear? I hope it's one of Conrad's hotels. Someplace nice?"

"The Astoria something or other," Zachary said.

"Alva's here with her charming friend, what's-his-name," Leslie said. "He asks about you."

"That's swell," Zachary said sarcastically.

When Leslie tried filling Zachary in on the details of Alva's assistant Henry, then young Arturo, the youth who'd served them the farewell dinner, Zachary begged off the line, though he was pleased that someone else knew Manny actually existed.

It's what Manny always did with pain. He put it in a separate compartment. He had done that through much of his life. Physical pain, emotional pain—it made little difference. He disassociated himself from it, put it aside. The cold had stopped. There was no emptiness now.

He felt small. Yes, yes, he was disappearing. He was so small.

"Are you ready to talk?"

The words echoed in the metal chamber but Manny heard: "Arf you eddie to walk?"

Manny couldn't make out the words, merely the sounds.

Earl Patrick spoke: "Bernard Manning, my little friend, we must have a conversation."

"Learned ganning, die little friend, we must save our nation."

Manny knew he was hallucinating. Perhaps he could struggle back to the words, struggle back from where he was going. He could use the words like rope, hang on to them. After all, that's what language had done for him all along. All he had to do . . ."

"Eggle spache deanin hobbler . . ."

16 Zachary spent the afternoon getting the young Mexican something to cover his half-naked body. The clothing not only served its proscribed purpose but also lifted Sali out of his funk. The two of them dined leisurely at a nearby outdoor café.

Zachary preferred some place with air-conditioning, but the youth, dressed in gray slacks, a fresh white shirt, and a thin, gold chain, wanted to dine out under the stars. Zachary suspected he not only wanted to see, but to be seen.

No longer the street urchin, Sali assumed the personality of a young, perhaps Spanish, aristocrat, heir to some mysterious fortune or title. Zachary found himself enjoying the young impostor. With his good looks, delicate features, glittering smile, impeccable manners, coyly expressive eyes, and remarkable command of English, the boy could pass. Yes, he could. He was a natural—a con artist who, with a little coaching, could climb easily among and beyond Leslie's circle of friends.

This wasn't the first time Zachary considered the idea of

taking Sali to America, but it was the first time he allowed it any serious consideration. Feeling safe now and having been comforted by a long soak in the tub, he felt good. Having had a fine meal, more wine than usual, and with only the starry night as cover, everything seemed possible.

He watched how easily the youth handled the knife and fork, how he dabbed the corners of his mouth with the cloth napkin. A bright chameleon like Sali would charm Leslie senseless. With a little tutoring, a university wasn't out of the question.

Zachary, having more than a sampling of surprisingly good wine on his palate, warmed to the role of a less domineering Professor Higgins. Sali had potential. Exposed to a more sophisticated life than he now knew, Sali would mature. He could succeed in anything he chose.

"How is it you speak English so well?"

"Could I stay the night?" Sali asked, clearly avoiding the question and obviously trying to forget he was to take the bus home this evening.

The sudden possibility of further intimacy bothered Zachary. Watching the boy prepare for his bath earlier was almost more than he could bear. Now, having had a few glasses of wine, Zachary was afraid that he might not be able to resist Sali's flirtations.

"Perhaps we should check the buses to Cuernavaca first," he said, trying to brush aside these momentary, luxurious, and no doubt ludicrous fantasies of his.

"I'll take care of that," Sali snapped. "There's one every hour, I'm sure. Your plane doesn't leave until tomorrow morning." The tone was adult, indulgent. "Now, can . . . may I stay with you?"

Zachary's emotions were sweeping by him like a barrage of shooting stars. He didn't want to part with Sali at all. Unfortunately, the longer the boy stayed the more difficult it would be to say good-bye. But he couldn't bring himself to say "no" directly. He couldn't bear to hurt the boy and Sali picked up on it.

"There are two beds in the room," Sali said, hiding a smile behind a sip of Zachary's wine.

"All right."

"I will sleep in one and you will sleep in one," Sali said, laughing and choking.

"I said it was all right. You don't accept 'yes' for an answer? The mark of a good negotiator, I'm told, is to know when he's already closed the sale."

"Yes. I'll accept 'yes.' It is a good answer. You will be in one bed and I shall be in one bed, that is the agreement. Then we'll both be in one bed, right?" Sali laughed.

"No more wine for you." Zachary turned, pretending to search for a waiter. He couldn't repress the smile.

Sali took one last sip from Zachary's glass.

Sali's depression seemed to come on as the night grew quiet and the small room seemed to close in on them. He stared out of the hotel room window. The building extended outward on both sides, forming a tunnel-vision view of the world outside. Despite its panoramic limitations, Sali was nonetheless intent upon looking at it.

Zachary, already in bed, opened his diary to the last entry. It was Sali's. If it had been anyone else's invasion, he would have ripped out the offending page. Instead, he smiled, then picked up his pen and began to write.

Dear Diary,

To borrow an already overborrowed phrase, it has been the worst of times and strangely, the best of times. . . .

Sali interrupted. "It's like a prison." He spoke dully. "No way out. Straight drop."

After staring at the page in his diary for a considerable length of time, Zachary knew there was nothing else he cared to say. The idea of keeping a journal never seemed more trivial, more self-indulgent. He closed the book, leaving the most dramatic and threatening situations of his life unrecorded. Perfectly appropriate, he thought.

The book, pen, and reading glasses went to the bedside table, a ritual of decades. "What a boring, old, habit-ridden sop I am," Zachary thought.

"Will you be up long?" Zachary asked the boy.

Sali didn't answer. He moved to the other bed, took off his shoes, then his shirt. Zachary turned away—a reticent voyeur.

When the bedclothes stopped rustling, Zachary reached up, and turned off the light.

"Good night," Zachary said.

"My name is Sali."

"I know. I read your note in my diary. My name is Zach. Good night, Sali."

The boy said nothing more.

Zachary closed his eyes with the thought that, tomorrow, it will all be over. The boy will be off to Cuernavaca. Zachary will be off to his humdrum life—a not quite happy ending to the nightmare, but an end just the same.

It was stuffy in the room. Zachary peeled off the blankets, then pulled the cotton sheet over him, more for security than warmth. However, he couldn't sleep. Perhaps it was the coffee. He strained to hear the regular rhythmic breathing of sleep from the other bed. He could not.

"Are you all right?" Zachary asked softly, so that he wouldn't wake Sali if he were sleeping.

"You asked me how I learned English," Sali said.

"That's right. And you didn't want to tell me."

"I have . . . I had a friend. He was an old man, a black man from your country. They killed him when they came for me."

"Oh . . . I'm very sorry, Sali."

"I like you to say my name. He taught me English, how to speak, how to read. We used to listen to music. Sometimes he would play for me something on his guitar. It was a place I could stay if I needed to. They killed him. Because of me. When they came to take me, he pulled a knife. Maybe they didn't know he was blind. Maybe they did."

"Who are they?"

"I don't know. I really don't know."

"What is it they want?"

There was a long silence. "He was my only friend."

"I wish I knew what to say."

"Zach, please let me come over and talk with you."

"Yes, of course."

Zachary heard the boy move from his bed, felt the weight upon the edge of his own. In the dim light, Sali's naked body had the form of an underexposed photograph, a mysterious beauty that was also frightening.

Sali reached for Zachary's hand, holding it in his.

"I guess I've been . . ." Sali searched for words.

"Quiet," Zachary said. "You've been very quiet or possibly, depressed."

"Yes, I guess. I'm not scared, exactly. But I feel very lonely."

Though he was not altogether certain of the boy's sincerity, he would give him the benefit of the doubt.

"Anybody would be after what you've been through. Things will get better." Zachary doubted his own sincerity. What he wanted to do was hold the boy, but he found himself imparting platitudes like a distant relative at a funeral.

"It's not that."

"What is it then? Do you know?"

"Your hand is cold," the boy took Zachary's hand, placing it between his thighs.

"No," Zachary said weakly.

"You think too much," the boy said, holding his hand there. "Feel."

It had been too long. How many years? When was the last time he had feelings like this? Don't think, he told himself. That's the problem. You're thinking. You are thinking about feeling. Zachary felt the sheets slipping off his body. Don't think. Feel. What he felt was shame. Where is Sali? Has he gone? Then Zachary realized his eyes were closed. How silly, he thought—like a two-year-old hiding his eyes so he cannot be seen.

Sali was beside him, looking into his eyes. It was then that Zachary realized that the breeze caressing his shoulders was not a breeze, but Sali's gentle petting.

"I want us to make love," Sali said.

"What?" Zachary said, begging for time to think. Don't think. Feel. What he meant to ask was, "why?" But that, too, would be silly.

Sali laughed. "What a funny question."

Sali moved closer and Zachary could feel their bodies touch, could feel Sali's breath on his face and his slender arms go around him and caress his back.

"You have shoulders like an armadillo," Sali said.

Sali had small, insistent hands. "Please," he whispered, his lips touching Zachary's ear.

"What?" Zachary almost swallowed the word.

"Relax."

"I'm sorry. Sali, this isn't . . ."

Sali's hands pressed against Zachary's neck. "When was the last time?"

"What?"

"When you were with someone?"

"How long ago?" Zachary regretted the stupidity of his questions, knew they were meant to keep the distance, postpone what now seemed inevitable. Sali's hands were gentle but insistent.

"People need food. People need sleep. People need to be touched, to feel," Sali said, embracing Zachary's shoulders, the boy's body pressing, warming Zachary.

How could I have come so far away, Zachary thought, how could I let myself do this? Be here. Don't think. Feel. The heat of the boy's body warmed him. He felt the slender, graceful body move against him. He believed if he allowed this to go on one moment longer, it would be too late. He would never return to . . . to what? He could not finish the thought. Something warm and firm pressed against his thigh.

Sali's fingers pressed against Zachary's lips. The boy spoke slowly, almost whispering. "At night," the boy said, "dogs and coyotes howl. You hear them? The sky is so big. So big. So big, it never stops. We are little dogs, little people. And we are lost. All of us. Sometimes we have to feel how lost we are before we can find another. Zachary, we need each other so we won't have to howl at the moon."

* * *

131

The scratching sound began to etch itself into Zachary's night-filled brain. It pulled him back from Sali's warm flesh.

"Be still," he said to the boy. Sali held his breath. The sound came from the window.

Sali saw it first. Zachary felt the boy's body go rigid. Zachary could make out a shape, the silhouette of a huge black shadow against the slightly lighter sky. It was a man.

"How?" Sali asked in an awed whisper.

Zachary figured the man used his legs and back as braces against the narrow walls and scaled the building step-by-step. Now he was prying open the window with his fingernails.

Sali slowly slid off Zachary, dropped quietly down the side of the bed and crawled across the floor toward the window.

"Sali?" Zachary whispered. "The windows open out."

"I know," Sali whispered as he inched himself up the wall below the figure clinging to the glass. He stood quickly and shoved the window open. The man disappeared silently. Zachary heard the man hit. It was like the sound a hand makes fluffing a pillow. Zachary got out of bed, started for the light.

"No. Leave it off," Sali said, still whispering. "Let's get out of here."

They dressed quickly.

Zachary alternated between stuffing his suitcase and putting on his shoes and socks. "Do you have any idea who it is we're killing?"

Sali checked the hallway outside.

"C'mon," he said in a hoarse whisper.

They chose the stairway, descending as quietly as they could.

"You want me to carry that?" Sali asked, referring to Zachary's suitcase.

"No." Zachary tried to pick up the distances, the repeating

geography of the stair steps in the dark, his free hand caressing the wall. It was so dark and the boy so quiet, Zachary had to get occasional verbal assurances Sali was still close.

"You're quite a sneak," Zachary said in the darkness.

"Thank you."

Zachary counted the landings to make sure they would be able to locate the lobby floor. He forgot about the missing thirteenth floor. Unlucky thirteen. They found themselves in the cellar. When they retraced their steps, they discovered the main floor was locked. They went back to the cellar which was little more than dimly lit by a bulb over a cistern.

They found a high cellar window, climbed onto some rickety shelves. Sali made it easily, first pulling Zachary's satchel, then Zachary.

Zachary cursed himself because his arms shook. No muscle. Just milk, he thought. Finally, he raised himself, using more bone than muscle. Zachary was amused. It seemed to him a "Laurel and Hardy" escape. He laughed. Sali laughed and said, *shush.*

The window led to an alley and the alley to the front. Zachary, in a sudden panic over his car keys, rummaged through his pockets, relieved when he finally found them.

When they passed the hotel entrance, Sali saw Earl Patrick in the lobby. Patrick faced away, toward the elevator. The desk clerk, obviously awake just for the inquiry, leaned over the counter, head in hands. There was another man, too—a Mexican, the one who held the knife at Sali's back.

After they passed the doorway, Sali said, "The fat man, he's after me. Not you."

"I think we're connected somehow." Zachary said. He turned to head toward the car, then stopped abruptly.

A third man, the American holding a walkie–talkie, stood by Zachary's tan Pinto.

"Well, so much for my lovely German engine."

"You take the car. Pick me up at the café. You know, where we ate. In five minutes," Sali said. With that he dislodged a brick from the crumbling mortar at the base of the building. "Stay here until the man is out of sight."

Sali, brick in hand, crouched and moved toward the car. He hurled the brick, crushing the walkie–talkie against the man's ear.

"Son of a bitch!" the man said, dropping his walkie–talkie and nearly falling.

Sali was almost out of sight before the injured man could respond.

"You little fucker," the man said breathlessly, running after Sali. As he ran, he put his hand on the wound. Feeling the blood, he screamed, "You little fucker!" into the darkness.

Zachary always had trouble with keys and locks. House keys. Car locks and ignitions. He saw Patrick huffing around the corner as he fumbled nervously at the door of the tan Pinto. The key engaged, the door opened, but Zachary couldn't get the key back out. Patrick slowed, smiled. He walked slowly toward Zachary.

Suddenly, Zachary managed to pull the key out. Now in the driver's seat, Zachary tried to find the ignition. Finally the key slipped in.

"Bless you," Zachary said. "Now, if you'll only start."

Patrick was at the driver's window, his big face peering in. A broad, jagged smile on his face.

The engine turned, instantly purring.

The man's fist came through the window as Zachary accelerated into the car ahead of him. Though his body lurched in a painful contortion, Patrick's hand remained on the wheel. Reverse. Zachary was doing his best with the wheel, banging this time into the car behind him.

With both hands, Zachary managed to overpower Patrick's grip and turn to the left. He accelerated, smashed into the rear bumper of the car in front. Complete stop. The engine stopped. Patrick no longer grinned. Zachary twisted the key. It sparked. But Patrick's massive hand clenched the back of Zachary's neck and Zachary felt as helpless as a rabbit in the clutches of a hawk.

Zachary found reverse, turned the wheels to the right and accelerated. The Pinto lurched backward onto the sidewalk. Patrick's arm was sucked back out of the broken window as quickly as it had come through.

First gear. Patrick was on his feet, but stunned, his shirt sleeve ripped to shreds and rippled with blood. Patrick's good hand went awkwardly across his body for his gun.

He got off one shot before dodging the charging Pinto.

17 "You're late," Sali said, getting in.

"Careful of the glass."

"What happened?"

"Your friend couldn't wait until I rolled the window down, so I nearly took his arm with me."

"He's not my friend," Sali said. "You're a pretty tough guy. Did Hoppy teach you that, too?"

"No. I learned to break things at an early age."

"Where are you going?" Sali asked as Zachary sped away.

"I don't know. Away from here. Let's just drive for a while until I can figure this thing out."

It was 4:00 A.M. Sometime between too early and too late. They drove the streets of a cool and quiet Mexico City.

"Shit," Sali said. "You know what?"

"What?"

"That bastard call me little."

"You're not exactly King Kong."

"The guy who chase me. Called me a 'little fucker,' a 'little son of a bitch.' Why didn't he call me a 'fucker' or 'son of a bitch.' No, he say 'little.' I hate that."

"You'll grow out of it."

"Maybe not," Sali said smiling, patting Zachary's thigh. "Maybe I'll always be a little fucker."

"The good thing about not knowing where we're going," Zachary said, changing the subject, "is that they won't either."

"Yes. And we won't be late," he giggled.

Zachary pulled to the side of the street, stopped the engine, and turned off the lights. Sali laid his head on Zachary's lap.

"Before you go off into the land of nod," Zachary said as he lifted the boy's head, "I want to know what this is all about. Why are they after you . . . me . . . us?

"I don't know." Sali's voice was suddenly small, emanating from the darkness.

"These people don't want me. Death is a pretty harsh punishment for a bad recipe."

"What?"

"Never mind. What did you do, besides kill a couple of people, or I should say, before you killed a couple of people, to make someone so determined to kill you. Me. Us."

"I think I had something somebody wants."

"What do you have and who wants it?"

"I don't know, exactly."

"Well, what inexactly?"

"I don't know."

"Yes, you do. I believe you do."

"Anyway, I don't have it anymore," Sali said.

"Who has it now?"

"Look," Sali said impatiently, "this friend of mine, he give . . . gave me something and told me to keep it until I meet this other person. I don't know who these people are. I know the big guy's a mean son of a bitch—a big fucker."

"I want to know," Zachary said harshly. "I want to know what I'm risking my life for."

"Maybe you risk it for . . ." his voice trailed off.

"What's wrong?"

"Nothing." His response was loud, but hoarse. He seemed about to cry.

"Where is this thing you're keeping a secret?"

"It's better you don't know."

"Sali, my life is on the line, too."

"That's why you should not know. If you do not know, you cannot tell. Because when you tell, they will kill you."

"C'mon, Sali."

"No. I cannot. I will tell you anything. I will do anything for you. But I cannot tell you anything more now."

Zachary heard the side door open. The interior light came on. Sali was leaving.

"Where are you going?"

Sali turned toward Zachary. His eyes were wet. "I'm going. You can fly back home. I can go to my uncle's house in Cuernavaca. Ditch the car. Buy some new clothes, new glasses. You can get out."

"Sali . . ."

"No. You helped me. I helped you. Friends?"

Sali held his hand out.

"Sali . . ."

"Friends. Shake?"

Zachary's stomach pitched.

"The least I can do," he said, "is drive you to your uncle's. Will you let me do that?"

* * *

Except for directions, for which he adopted a formal tone, Sali was quiet on the way to Cuernavaca. Sali directed Zachary to a house in a run-down suburb.

Squinting in the sun, Sali said, "Good luck, my friend."

It took Zachary forever to work out of the maze of this part of town and find a road that was clearly marked on the map. The moment he found the highway and no longer had to think about it, his mind turned back to Sali. Was this love he was feeling?

"Jeremiah," the thin, balding Senator Hedges said kindly as he stood to greet Jeremiah Tower.

"Robert."

"Train?"

"Yes. Not a bad way to travel . . ." Tower said. Both sat down. "If one is to go all the way to Baltimore for lunch."

"This is a fine restaurant, Jeremiah." Senator Hedges slipped on his half-frame reading glasses and opened the menu, then peered over them to stare directly into Tower's steely eyes: "Afterward, perhaps we can walk down by the bay. Soak up a little American history."

"We could have soaked up quite a bit of American history in Washington. But then, of course, we might run into somebody we know. Isn't that right, Senator Hedges?"

"I've no doubt you're clever, Jeremiah. Trying to prove the obvious causes doubts."

"And what does a clever man order here?" Tower nudged his menu to the edge of the table.

"Not the crab cakes."

"I've never been fond of crab. Too cautious. They bury themselves in the sand."

"There is a time to move and a time to stay still. My grand-daddy used to say . . ."

"Save it for C-Span. I've never really savored your brand of folksy wisdom, Senator Hedges."

"I don't imagine you do," Hedges said, giving Tower a squinting look. "And I don't imagine you much savorin' a word to the wise from just plain folks." He paused for a moment.

Tower looked away.

"I'd recommend the tuna. It's freshly caught," Hedges said. "That reminds me. Did you ever see that cartoon? I think it was in *The New Yorker* where this little fish was about to be gobbled up by a bigger fish and the bigger fish was about to be gobbled up by an even bigger fish, and so on?"

"No. I can't say I remember seeing it. You say it was a cartoon?"

"*Umm hmm.* Just a cartoon. But it sorta says that if you're not the biggest fish in the lake, maybe you don't want to do a lot of wigglin' and a lot of splashin' when the big fish are hungry."

"And are the big fish hungry, senator?"

"Yeah. Mighty appetite."

When Manny awoke again, he had some semblance of sanity about him. The sleep had been good. How long he had slept was another question, one he couldn't answer. But he was now almost lucid and he had enough strength to move. Perhaps it was something akin to getting a second wind.

Again, he paced the tank. Again, he found the small holes where once a ladder had been. Immediately, he went to his blanket. It was still damp. He tore it into six strips. He took one and tied a knot at the end. Manny stuck the knotted end into one of the holes, the highest one he could reach, and jerked on it. It held.

Did he have enough strength to do what he needed to do? Enough for one small burst of energy? Maybe. His life depended upon it. Manny did the same thing with each strip of blanket—tiny knots that when pulled upon, lodged in the small holes. Manny pulled himself up with the first strip to put in the second. Then the third. Now he was able to pull himself to the top.

Manny paused for a moment before trying it. He took three deep breaths, then climbed up the side of the tank. He pushed. He pushed again. The hatch at the top was locked. Of course.

"We've gone for your little walk, now get to the point, Senator Hedges," Jeremiah Tower said, glaring at the bespectacled senator who stared out into Baltimore Harbor.

"*Mmm.* Yes. The point is a computer chip. Seems as if the company you're working for is competin' against the government. Our government, Mr. Tower. Since when is a private company . . ."

"Senator Hedges, if I were you . . ."

"I know," the Senator interrupted. "Let me say it for you. If you were me you'd be very careful so as not to suffer from a heart attack while sleepin' some night. Is that right? Of course, I'm sure you have other ways. But I'm clean, Tower. Squeaky clean. You won't find my name on a prostitute's list and you'll never see me in the Chesapeake Club. I take no PAC money and being from my little state, believe it or not, I've not even been offered a bribe, let alone accepted one. Some say I'm beyond original sin."

"How Christian."

"That, too. This little junket is on record with two other members of Congress who share my concerns about private government and sovereign power for chairmans of corporations."

"No private agendas except your own, right? Listen, if I do anything, it is to take care of the business your bloated, ineffectual, self-interested body of the government can't. If I do anything, it's to take care of the business the emasculated, old-maid bureaucracy can't. As much as I find you distasteful, Senator Hedges, we really believe in the same things. It's just that one of us does something about it."

"Send your folks home, Tower. The chip belongs to us. It's a matter of national security."

"Like most of the so-called gentlemen of Congress, you're a very small man, a petty bureaucrat who soaks up the trappings of his office as if you really had a place in history. Country bumpkins like you run for office because you couldn't make it in the business world, not even in the small towns you come from."

"Tower, fold up shop. Get your inept people out of Mexico. Keep getting your government research grants, write your columns, and let your distinguished face grace the bookflaps. Your time for meddling with the security of this country is up. We don't want the embarrassment of still more hearings any more than you do."

"Make your charges public or leave me alone." Tower turned, walked back up toward the street.

"Tower," the senator said, "we're closin' you down right now, as we speak."

Tower, not wanting his name shouted all over the harbor, turned, walked halfway back to the senator. He glared at the senator.

"You have absolutely no class, whatsoever."
"What we do have is Bernard Manning."
"I never heard of him," Tower said.
"Oh?"
"You may kill him for all I care."

18

Zachary drove like a man who wanted to leave his newfound feelings behind, but he couldn't escape them entirely. Would Sali be safe? Couldn't they trace him? If those bastards were that good—good enough to find the two of them in the middle of Mexico City, then couldn't they locate someone in Puerto Vallarta who could key them into an uncle in Cuernavaca? Couldn't they be there already?

All of this was just a rationale to return, Zachary argued. Face it, old Zach. It's lust. Desire. Pure emotional, adolescent-styled lust. And it didn't look good on a man approaching middle-age. Where's the future in that? You don't want to get into all that again. Your life has been . . . well . . . adequate.

Zachary swerved to miss an armadillo. The car spun. The landscape whirled. Zachary clutched the wheel and crushed the brake. The car stopped. Engine dead. Silence. There was nothing around him but parched grass, a harsh, almost white sky, and the armadillo. The armadillo stood his ground, staring.

How long would Sali be content with him, once the city beckoned? Disappointment. His. Sali's. Why create hope? Hadn't he learned how treacherous the path of expectation was? He was content without love, involvement. God knows, he'd learned to live without sex. Wasn't that the goal? Purging desire in all its manifestations? He had, hadn't he, except for the small extravagances that he could, in fact, afford? Hadn't he had his peace? His contentment. He had that. Why go where there is pain and regret? You've done it. You've severed the ties. It was painful, but it was done. Why undo it? It would just mean more pain later.

Zachary closed his eyes. He must regain his composure. He must think.

Don't think. Feel.

Jeremiah Tower couldn't resist traveling by train when the opportunity presented itself. When he left Senator Hedges, Tower grabbed a taxi for the Baltimore train station and boarded the Metroliner for D.C. Trains were less stressful than automobiles—he hated to drive anyway—and they were far more comfortable than traveling by air, unless it was aboard his own jet.

He pulled a copy of Wolfe's *Bonfire of the Vanities* out of his briefcase. Tower always held a bit of competitive animosity toward New York and for a while, swore he wouldn't read the book. But he had read more and more about Wolfe and found himself having a sort of begrudging admiration for the writer's political beliefs.

He forced his way through the nonsensical first chapter and settled in comfortably soon enough, glancing up every once in awhile to look out the window at what Tower referred to "as the ass-end of East Coast cities."

These scrap yards, boarded-up factories, decaying neighborhoods, and rusted fences gave credence to his belief that the United States had moved beyond redemption. A new order was required, and as far as he was concerned, under way. In the new order, the government—no longer able to afford or provide the expertise to preserve an effective government—had to yield to a governing body made up of international corporate entities with proven management records and an understanding of the global economy. That was the essence of the new order. It was the only way the world could work.

Tower's agitation over Senator Hedges's threats soon gave way to humor. The Congress had long ago given away its right to indignation. And its petty and ineffectual battles with the executive branch were just that. The greedy Congress had been purchased as well, if for nothing else, to get or keep their seats.

And Tower had to laugh at Hedges's claim that his people had Bernard Manning. His people? Which of the alphabet bureaucracies were providing the clandestine muscle on this one? Sooner or later Hedges's people would be Tower's people. The senator and his friends in Congress were as much in control of this country's destiny as its citizens were, the sad majority who paid the corporations who bought Congress and the presidency. It was Congress who needed to be eliminated. Oh well, he thought, England had its queen. America had its Congress. Secret government. Yes, thank goodness. A secret government was better than no government at all.

However, this little Mexico mess was in danger of blowing up. As important as it was, Tower wasn't about to lose the kingdom for the want of a computer chip. He would simply obliterate the trail and if the prize turned up in the process, so much the better. The order was in.

With his arm bandaged, a three-hour nap at a roadside inn, and breakfast, Earl Patrick drove his big Caprice down the narrow highway. He was ready to put an end to what he could put an end to. That would be Bernard Manning. The fag writer and the wetback kid were somebody else's problem now.

What would he do? Shoot him? Climb down and break his neck? Not with his arm the way it was. Maybe he would fill the tank with water and let the smart-ass drown? Not a bad idea. No blood. The body would float to the top. He'd pull it out and tie a rock to it and toss it overboard. Quick. Easy. Something he could do with his bad arm.

What Earl Patrick would do when he got back would be to sit down, have a cigarette on the gently bobbing tanker, look out to sea, and contemplate Bernard Manning's eminent demise.

There was nothing now to get from him. He had nothing. To let him live was to invite the real possibility of his own death, or at best, someone to testify against him. Use your own judgment, was the advice he was given. "Just make it tidy," were the words used.

The neighborhoods were a mystery to Zachary, whose eyes were more often used to discriminate the difference between well-ripened olives and poorly ripened ones than discovering the subtleties of Cuernavaca's suburbs. Every house looked alike. Zachary looked for the trace of bright yellow he had seen in the front window. Perhaps Sali would be outside. Perhaps the world would end today.

The sun was intense. Zachary's upper lip was moist. Sweat

burned his eyes and the sun blinded them, and the fucking white houses all looked alike, and the streets all looked alike, and the people all looked alike. It was an impossible task.

What else about the house? The door was in the middle. The house was symmetrical. Red clay roof. They all had fucking red clay roofs. White house, red roof, and no grass on the lawns. Lawns. Pink flowers. *Jesus Christ, this is crazy,* he thought. It was a bush of pink flowers on the right side. Yes, the house was more colorful than the rest. Neater. Yellow in the window. Pink in the yard.

He found the house. No, it wasn't it. Perhaps it was. He parked the car, walked up the path. It didn't seem to be right, but it had yellow curtains and a pink bush.

"No, *señor.*"

He told them he was looking for a young boy. Sali, he told them. They stood shaking their heads, the man and woman. Shaking heads and sad eyes. For a moment, Zachary thought they were telling him the boy was dead, that Sali was not there because he was dead. But it was not the house. It was not the aunt and uncle. The uncle was fatter, the aunt was shorter.

He got in his car. He drove. He looked at the young Mexican boys. Every one who bore the least resemblance to Sali was viewed with anticipation, anxiety, despair.

If he could only find something familiar. Some tree, rock, twist in the street, a bit of tile on a porch step. That was it. There was tile on the doorstep. A blue-green pattern with traces of yellow. And the yellow draperies and the pink flowers and the fat uncle and the short aunt.

How many millions of people lived in Mexico City–Cuernavaca? More than New York. More than Tokyo. Christ. But Zachary knew he was in the right area. He had backtracked and he knew where he was going until he got here. So, maybe the population was narrowed down to a few million. No, his odds were better than that.

After an hour of wrong turns, false recognitions, and a constant flood of perspiration, Zachary found it. Zachary pushed the horn. No Sali. But this was definitely his aunt. He recognized the gold tooth, the gentle eyes. He was sorry he had been so rude as to honk and have this woman come to him. Zachary said, "pardon." It was as close as he could get to something that might come close to an apology. He asked about Sali.

Peering through the passenger side, the aunt said something he interpreted as "town."

In the darkness, Manny could hear the noise. There was a fumbling at the grate above him. There was a thin sliver of light and a curse. It was Earl Patrick's gravelly voice. Using the knotted strips of blanket, Manny quickly pulled himself up to the top. Then suddenly, blindingly, the light hit him. He couldn't see. It was a split second of panic. Manny had neglected to consider the impact of sudden light.

"What the fuck . . ." Earl Patrick's voice exploded.

Without thinking, without knowing exactly what he was grabbing for, Manny reached up, felt something in his grasp— Patrick's tie—and yanked while he pressed himself against the wall of the tank. He felt Patrick's body hit him as the big man tumbled in. Now, Manny was falling. Blind fall. Soft landing. His body had landed on Patrick's.

Manny got to his feet, ready to fight. But he heard no movement. His eyes were getting accustomed to the light.

There was no doubt about it. A severed tongue, a broken neck. Earl Patrick was very ugly and very dead.

* * *

When Sali's aunt went back in the house, her husband came out. Zachary declined the uncle's invitation to come inside. Instead he sat in the car, half-sleeping in the heat of the afternoon sun and retracing the events that had brought him here.

The fat lady who wanted the sea to swallow her, the dead fish with glazed eyes, the woman floating in the pool, Manny's strange disappearance, his own near-death, three times. All the violence. All the death. He wondered if he were in time, if Sali had already been abducted or killed. What was this thing everyone wanted? How was it, they—whoever they were—always knew where to find them?

The dream was the same. Zachary was alone in the plaza. This time there were people. But he was unable to speak and he was unable to understand the language of the strangers. He did not know who or where he was. He was without a past, a future, a purpose. There was a crow . . . moving so close. . . .

Zachary felt something soft, moist against his cheek. He awakened with a jerk to see Sali's smiling face.

"You're early," Sali said. "I figure you come back tomorrow."

19

"Why don't you just call the police, Zach?" said the slightly lisping voice coming over the phone.

In the lobby of a shabby hotel in Cuernavaca, at a pay phone, Zachary held a hand against his ear to hear Leslie's distantly weak voice through the static and the conversation at the check-in desk.

"It's not possible. There's the boy, Sali. I've got to get him out of here, too."

"I can't imagine dear, cautious Zachary, how you could have gotten yourself in such a fix. By the way, Alva Burdine says to tell you everything will be all right. She's very worried."

"That's very nice, but . . ."

"She's worried sick."

"I hardly know her."

"That reminds me, I must call her. What's all this nasty business about? Drugs?"

"I haven't the faintest idea. All I know is what I told you. There are murders and chases and . . ."

"Where's our fearless crusader? Your adventurous Boy Wonder?"

"I don't know, Leslie. He's part of a strange puzzle. He's missing."

"Voluntarily?"

"I told you, I don't know."

"Seems as if you know very little of anything. Are you sure you're not just overcome by the heat?"

"Leslie, please. No more chitchat. This is urgent. The question is, can you get us out of here? You have some rich connections. . . ."

"Can't you just fly out like any other ordinary human being? If you've run out of money . . ."

"I told you, Leslie. I can get out. But there's the boy." Zachary looked to see if anyone was listening. "No passport. Nothing."

"Why don't you just give the boy a couple of thousand pesos or so. By the sound of it, I'm sure he can take care of himself. Probably better than you can. I don't know why you didn't go to Europe."

"Leslie, are you going to help me or not?"

"Well, dear boy, let me try. If your little friend isn't an unsurpassed beauty, I shall be extremely disappointed. After all, your original traveling companion may have been a bit testy, but he wasn't without his charm. Testy and tasty. I can't wait until you come back. You remember Arturo? Our handsome waiter at the farewell dinner? He's writing a novel. Isn't that charming? He told me so as he lay wrapped in those ivory silk sheets I have for such special occasions."

"Leslie, please." Thinking about Leslie and Arturo as he

looked at Sali standing thumbing through a magazine by the door made him feel dirty. He felt a sudden distaste for his neighbor and himself. "Yes or no?"

"I don't know how long this will take. Where are you staying?"

"I'll call you in the morning."

"Just your phone number, Zachary, in case I need to talk with you earlier."

"Maybe the phones are tapped."

"Dear boy. . . ."

"Thank you, Leslie. There was no one else I could turn to." *Click.*

"What do we do now?" Sali asked, as they walked up the steps to the room. The desk clerk's radio blared "Total Eclipse of the Heart."

"I guess we wait until morning. Leslie . . . a friend of mine, may be able to get us out of here. Back to the States."

"Us?"

"I'm to call him in the morning, if we survive another night." Zachary gave a small, inward laugh.

Sali was quiet. He stretched across the bed, his head resting on his forearm.

Zachary checked the window. It was barred. No one could get in; but no one could get out, either. Perhaps, he thought, they should have just continued to drive. If he and Sali were discovered here, there was no exit and most certainly whoever was after them would not be so careless next time.

He went into the bathroom. One narrow window, not large enough for a body to pass through. He looked in the mirror. Despite the harsh light and the lack of either sleep or a shave, he looked well. Younger, even.

"Are you tired?" Zachary asked, entering the room.

"No."

"What's wrong?"

"Why didn't you ask me if I wanted to go to America?"

"You don't want to go?" Zachary sat down on the edge of the bed and touched Sali's shoulder.

"Sure, every Mexican wants to go to America," Sali said bitterly.

"I'm not following, Sali. What do you mean?"

"I had a friend," Sali said, "who smothered to death in the trunk of a car packed with Mexicans crossing the border."

"I still . . ."

"He was on the bottom. His body was all burned by the tail pipe and he couldn't even scream. He burned and smothered . . ."

"I'm sorry," Zachary said.

"It's the way it's supposed to be, isn't it? No one, not even the Mexicans want Mexico. They want a Chevy and to make it big in America," Sali said, sitting. "But nobody does, do they? They end up as somebody's cleaning woman? What can I be? You want me to be your houseboy?"

"Sali . . ."

"Yes, I want to go. But you didn't ask. We didn't talk like two . . . friends. Because I am too young? Because I am a Mexican? Because I'm not equal to you in some way?"

"Because if we stayed, we'd be killed," Zachary said, standing up and walking to the window.

"I can take care of myself," Sali said. He got off the bed, turned off the overhead light. He kicked off his shoes and began to unbutton his shirt in the dim glow of the nightstand lamp.

Bare-chested and shoeless, Sali sat back on the edge of the

bed. "Why I want to go . . . the only reason I want to go is because I want to be with you."

Zachary was quiet. He knew he wasn't being honest with Sali. He did love him. Could he tell him? Did Zachary have the right to inflict his middle-aged anxieties on someone whose life was all before him? Sali was entitled to know what he was getting into. Loving required that.

Wouldn't Sali wake up one day and begin to recognize Zachary's inevitable slide into eccentricity? Or insanity? Infirmity? Senility? Christ, Zachary thought, he was scaring himself. But wasn't it true that Sali would have to come to know all the old ghosts of Zachary's life? Ones that even he preferred to forget and had, pretty successfully, for years?

Wasn't it a case of one life winding down and the other just beginning? How fair was that? No, he could not allow it.

Or, was it something else? Something less noble. Would Zachary jeopardize his comfortable privacy? Would he make himself vulnerable one more time? Wasn't that it? After all, hadn't he learned to be a turtle? To carry his walls with him? Hadn't he adjusted to making his way alone? Frightened, maybe, but not showing it. Friendly, sociable conversation, offering a bit of wit, but little else, certainly no feeling.

Hadn't he lived vicariously, avoiding the risk of personal relationships? Hadn't he avoided human error? True. Hadn't he avoided being human? True, too.

"When I was young, about nineteen," Zachary said, sitting back down on the bed beside Sali, "a big black bird called to me one day and made me see the truth."

Sali stiffened. His laugh was bitter.

"Now you are going to tell me a little boy story? Then I can kneel, say my prayers, and go to sleep like a good little boy. Fuck you."

Zachary had to get his breath, recover. He felt as if he'd been slapped.

"No, no wait a minute," he said calmly. "This is true. It was in Michigan. In the snow. That's when the bird came. Be patient. I had met someone. We fell in love. We were so in love that we spent the first three days we knew each other in bed. It wasn't just sex, though there was plenty of that. We slept and dreamed. It was like our bodies, our minds, perhaps our souls had become entwined.

"We couldn't bear to be apart. As the days followed, even though we started to move around and eat and do normal things, we continued to drift into each other. We shared everything it is conceivable to share. Every thought, every desire, every act of consequence no matter how perverse, normal, innocent, knowing, or cruel. Every lie, every fear.

"It didn't take long before he became the reason I lived. We moved in together—at his insistence, oddly, as it turned out. Then gradually, something happened. I don't know what it was, or why. David began to stay away longer and later. He became increasingly distant, impatient, cold.

"Of course, I didn't realize it at the time, but the further he went away, the closer I tried to get, which in turn sent him further away. At night I'd crawl closer to him, unconsciously perhaps, until he moved to the couch, and then finally out of the apartment.

"I became his unwanted possession. He held my soul and, whether he wanted to or not, he couldn't give it back. Finally, there was a confrontation. He said it was over. I didn't fight it. I couldn't. There wasn't any person inside me to object.

"I can't tell you how lost I was. The very thing I waited my life to find, I found. Then it went away. There was nothing I could do about it. And I didn't care whether I lived or died. I was pretty sure I was already dead."

"So what about this bird?" Sali asked, still suspicious.

"One day, I finally got up enough whatever to go withdraw from my classes. I had already missed them anyway, sleeping as much as I could, crying, and sitting like a zombie the rest of the time. I walked through the woods on the way to the university and I heard this loud screech. I heard the screech like it was inside my head. I looked up. I saw a big, black bird. It flapped its wings and flew away."

"Yes," Sali said, as if he knew what Zachary was going to say next.

"And for some very strange, inexplicable reason, it seemed like I could see for the first time. I know that sounds strange. But it was like I could see in a new way, or maybe the old way before I became lost in someone else's soul. Suddenly things were clear in a way they never had been before. I saw the trees, laden with snow for the first time, though it had been that way for days, weeks. I heard the crunch of snow under my feet. I could feel the cold in my nostrils and in my throat. I saw the stark, black, naked limbs of the trees reaching for the silver sky. An entire season had changed and I hadn't noticed until then. More though, I suddenly had a momentary, and, for me, profound understanding . . . that nothing is permanent.

"It's true," Sali said.

"It is perhaps good to know that. Perhaps it is also unfortunate. It changed me, Sali. I fear ever getting lost again. I am a coward. I don't want to love. I don't want to risk it."

"Maybe I'm your black bird," Sali said. "You know, the black bird that says come with me? Maybe it's time to change again."

"Sali, it's too late. Too late to start."

"No. Don't tell me that . . ." Sali stood up, unbuttoned his gray slacks and slid them down.

Zachary turned away.

Sali moved in front of him. He touched Zachary's cheeks. Zachary started to speak. *"Shhh,"* Sali said. "Look at me."

The plane would bring them back to San Francisco, Leslie said on the phone the next morning.

Zachary and Sali followed instructions. They said good-bye to the Pinto at the landing strip, not too far from Cuernavaca. There was a man, a Mexican, in a dark-blue suit standing beside a gray Plymouth Valiant. It was an old car, but it looked official.

The man motioned for them to come over. He held a walkie–talkie in his hand. Zachary could hear the static twenty feet away.

"Ask him how long before the plane . . ." Zachary said to Sali.

"I can speak English," the man said. "About ten minutes."

Zachary was curious. For an out-of-the-way place, the landing strip was pretty impressive—very well kept and stretching as far as he could see. Yet there were no buildings. None. A secret government spot, or maybe a place where high-placed drug lords smuggled their illicit goods?

The ten minutes seemed like an afternoon. Finally, Sali pointed to the distant silver cross descending from the sky. Zachary checked his watch. Nine minutes. The plane swept down, landed in the distance, and moved toward them, the heat distorting its image so that the surprisingly small craft shimmered dreamily, like some exotic, futuristic bird-beast.

The man walked the two of them to the door. Zachary with his luggage. Sali, awed, behind him. No words were exchanged. Sali and Zachary climbed the steps and entered the plush cabin.

No sooner had the man shut the door than the plane began to taxi, turn, and begin the rush before liftoff.

Sali was big-eyed and breathing heavily. He was so transfixed at the land rushing by the window, he didn't notice Zachary buckle him in.

"The least they could do is provide a magazine," Zachary said, laughing. He felt great relief. The liftoff threw his head back against the pillow. He thought it strange the pilot didn't make introductions or talk about flight times or tail winds. Perhaps he had been engaged in a more pleasurable pursuit when he was ordered to make the emergency airlift.

After all, Zachary had no idea who Leslie had contacted, what favor he'd called in, or promised, to provide the means of escape.

20

Manny was exhausted and he could do little more than sit down beside the corpse in the little pool of light. He had never, since he was a kid in grade school, struck someone else. Now he had killed a man. He felt as if he'd lived twenty years in the last—what—how many hours? Days? It didn't make any difference. He felt older, but not a bit wiser.

He was free. He could go now. Where, exactly, was more than a little puzzling at the moment. He was no longer frightened of losing his life or his mind, both distinct possibilities only moments ago. He was frightened, though. He was sure he could climb up out of the hole. He could. He could do that. For what? For whom? It was just a bigger hole out there. He wouldn't be any less alone, would he? That much was clear now.

"Mom, Dad, I'm home," he said out loud. "Yeah, right. Why don't the two of you come visit me and my charming wife and my two lovely children in Milwaukee." He laughed. "We'll barbecue some steaks and I'll tell you how my job is going. I'll introduce you to my friends," he said, poking the body laying in front of him. "This is my friend, Harold. Wasn't it nice of him to drop in?"

Manny felt Patrick's jacket and pulled out a wallet from the breast pocket. He opened it.

"Oops," he said. "Earl Jones Patrick." It wasn't the guy's name that troubled Manny. He'd never heard of him. It was the set of initials beside the name, the three little letters which identified Patrick's employer. They weren't the same three little letters which identified Manny's employer, but they came from the same alphabet.

Manny looked up at the little hole of bright light. He was now fully aware of the darkness that surrounded him. He suddenly became aware of his nakedness. He felt cold, very cold. So cold his teeth chattered.

For maybe an hour, Sali looked out of the window, obviously taken with a view of the world he'd never seen before. After several minutes with nothing but clouds to gaze at, he turned back to Zachary.

"You tell me you're a cook," Sali said, looking quite serious, Zachary thought. "And you have this big plane come all the way to Mexico just for you."

"And you," Zachary said.

"It does not make sense."

"I agree with you. It doesn't make sense. But it doesn't matter anymore. We're safe and whatever that nightmare was about, it's over."

"There are things you are not telling me," Sali said.

"I'm afraid I've finally leveled with you, Sali. But there are some things you are not telling me."

"You got me, Hoppy," Sali said, turning quietly back to the window.

The whole idea of settling back into his condo, his neighborhood, his rituals, gave Zachary not only a feeling of security but an even greater appreciation of his life before these bizarre days in a strange land.

He was, however, still confused about Sali. It's not that he wanted the boy out of his life—far from it. The decision had been made. That, however, didn't lessen his confusion about it all. How could they ever have a relationship? What kind of relationship could it be with someone so young and someone who was approaching middle age at the speed of light? What did they have in common?

One was a somewhat effete, reclusive, asexual human being who preferred to fuss about a kitchen and write esoteric recipes with an expensive pen rather than engage in the passion, rages, disappointments, and struggles of the majority of the population.

The other was a young, vital, adventurous, street-wise urchin at the prime of his sexual being who knew nothing but the struggle to survive and the gratification of basic needs.

Though social engagements were low on Zachary's agenda, there were some. There were trips to be made from time to time. How did Sali fit in? Would Sali come along or be left at home, cut off from the rest of Zachary's life, meager as it was? It would have been difficult before to introduce anyone as his lover. Now, with Sali, it was unthinkable. Who could understand? Certainly, he didn't. Even more certainly, he would not have looked kindly on anyone else involved in such a situation. The word "pedophile" crossed his mind and Zachary shuddered.

How old was Sali? Eighteen, did he say? Maybe. He didn't

look it. Even so, Zachary was almost old enough to be the boy's grandfather.

Conflicting and confusing emotions passed through Manny's brain during the hour he sat beside Earl Patrick's corpse. Futility, then anger. A recognition of some sort of perverse humor in the universe. Then futility again.

"Be rational," he said out loud. "You have a choice. Go or stay. If you do not choose 'go,' then you have chosen 'stay.' If you stay very much longer," he continued to talk out loud, "then, without food and water, you will not have the strength to go and you will be here slowly going insane, not to mention slowly dying next to a rotting corpse who wasn't too pretty to begin with. Okay, go.

"All right, what's next, genius? Is something or someone preventing you from going? No sounds on deck. No one has peered down through the hole. You must assume the way is clear. What next? You need clothes." He looked down at the clothing that covered the rather large body next to him and decided that they would have to do if there were nothing else.

As he undressed the body, for a moment he thought of leaving Mr. Patrick naked as he himself had been abandoned. But the thought of seeing this man out of his underwear was less than inspiring; and so he left Earl Patrick in his urine-stained boxers.

Wallet? Keys? Money? An American Express card, maybe? Passport? Manny checked the wallet again. Yes, money. More than enough. Green gringo dollars and multicolored pesos. An American Express. A picture of some woman. Thank God, no kids. A Social Security card. "Sorry, Mr. Patrick. A bad investment." There was an international driver's license. No good. The photo. A pair of cheap aviator-style sunglasses. Two insurance cards—medical and automobile. Two frequent-flyer cards. A membership in a video club in Cleveland.

The guy had a life. Manny would rather have left the guy's life in a single dimension. In Patrick's pants pocket there were some pesos and American coins. There was a hotel key, a key to a rental car—the tag said, "black Caprice" and gave the license number—and a package of chewing gum. Manny wrapped everything but the chewing gum in the clothing, rolled them into a tight ball, fastened by the belt, and after a few attempts, managed to successfully toss them through the hole and onto the deck above.

Manny put two pieces of gum in his mouth and felt not only a small rush of energy but an incredible feeling of hunger. That in itself was motivation enough to climb out. His eyes blanched at the sunlight.

"What? Again?" he said, as he struggled, naked as a new-born, out of the dark hole.

Zachary, though he was terrified of takeoffs and landings, didn't mind flying. However, no matter how smooth the flight, he had never been able to truly rest while his body was in motion. He wished he had thought of picking up something to read—anything. But he hadn't exactly departed from a TWA terminal.

He closed his eyes. The sound of the plane was a mere hum. There were many things Sali could do in San Francisco, Zachary thought, as his head was forced back against the headrest. There were the parks like Buena Vista, where from the green hill they could look out over much of the city. The great restaurants of North Beach. The wharf and the ferry to Sausalito. San Gregorio beach—that vast stretch of sand below the wall of rock, a beach unlike any in Mexico.

The department stores on Union Square—Macy's and Saks and Neiman-Marcus and down the street, Nordstrom. The bakeries, Il Forneo. The movie houses, the grand hotels. The museums. Perhaps even the opera. It would be exciting for Sali.

He would take Sali to the great parade on Chinese New Year. And they would wander the deserted streets of Chinatown after the parade, when all that was left was the smell of spent fireworks and the fog that seemed to rise from the wet, brick streets. The two of them would walk in the Oriental night, bathed in pink from indecipherable neon signs.

He looked over at Sali, who was sleeping, his head resting against the window, his beautiful face expressionless. Behind the now soiled white shirt, Sali's chest rose and fell steadily. The youth's hand rested inches away from Zachary's knee as if having fallen just slightly short of its attempted destination.

Topside, Manny found Patrick's clothes. They had landed in a puddle of oily water. He fumbled through them and found nothing worth salvaging. The thought occurred to him that someone had gone back to the hotel room and that fueled his concerns about Zachary. Had they harmed him? Or had he helped them? No way he could get an answer to that now. Manny thought he might never have an answer.

He found some musty, rubber rain gear, some oversized boots, some tins of tuna and bottled water. He sat on a pile of rope, wisely taking small sips of water, and only a quarter of the can of the tuna he had pried open with a rusty screwdriver.

Manny thought about taking Patrick's Caprice. It was parked on the dock. But he didn't know how many others were around and how easily the car would be recognized. He felt stronger anyway and believed he could walk back to town where he would cautiously inquire about his traveling companion. He'd take a room in any event.

In the heavy, dark, rubber raincoat and high-topped, black, rubber boots, Manny got more than a few stares as he walked in blazing sunlight to the center of Puerto Vallarta. He was a sickly, pale-faced zombie who looked as if he'd been dredged from the sea. He felt like he was in one of those Fellini movies Zachary had rented.

The desk clerk didn't recognize him and at first wanted nothing to do with the bizarre man whose haunting green eyes peered from the haggard, stubbled face. The offering of an obscene quantity of pesos made the man more charitable and he explained that Zachary Grayson had checked out days ago. No, the man had said, no one had accompanied him.

More pesos and the clerk provided a room and expressed his willingness to see that Manny got some new clothes, a razor, shaving cream, a toothbrush, toothpaste, deodorant, and a comb. The clerk was downright friendly as he wrote down his guest's requirements and sizes for the new wardrobe. He promised to get the toilet articles immediately, as well as food and several bottles of water.

Manny took a long, hot shower. Looking in the mirror afterward wasn't encouraging. He looked pale where before he had the beginning of a tan. Cheeks sunken beyond the fashionable, he imagined he could be Horatio's skull in Hamlet's hand. On the other hand, Suzie on Stanyan Street would no longer find the pudgy belly if, in fact, he ever found Suzie again.

He sat down on the edge of the bed and dialed Zachary's San Francisco number. He let it ring twenty times before giving up, then tried to remember his neighbor Leslie's last name. That futile reverie was broken by a young man delivering food, toiletries, and Manny's garish new clothes.

Clean and full, Manny slept. If his unappreciative employers or dangerous and mysterious adversaries happen to find him there, Manny wouldn't care. At least he'd die with a full stomach.

The sun was now below the clouds as Zachary felt the jet reduce its altitude and, within seconds, make its way toward hundreds of little blue lights faintly glowing along the runway in the eerie salmon light of the falling sun. The tires touched the runway, then the plane rose, then touched again, and the engines revved.

"Are we there?" Sali asked, bleary-eyed.

"Yes," Zachary said. He wondered why he didn't feel a greater sense of relief at being home. Perhaps it was just his usual nervousness at landing, or maybe it was the strange, isolated feeling he always had during the dusk hours.

The plane taxied, turning off the runway, and away from the main terminal. It moved to a relatively small metal hangar. Sali and Zachary disembarked inside the building. Leslie was not there to meet them. Instead they were met by a man in a gray suit, who said nothing, merely led them to a Mercedes limousine with tinted windows and a glass partition between the passengers and driver, a man whom they could not see and who said nothing to them.

Both Zachary and Sali were nervous and quiet, but Zachary felt a little easier when the car hit the San Francisco exit to the highway. They were heading for the city.

Zachary felt a genuine lift in spirits when he'd passed the ball park, passed the lights of the homes on the hillsides, and saw the wonderful skyline come suddenly into view. For the first time, he looked at that miniature Manhattan and didn't mind the high-rises. Nor did he mind one of the poorer parts of the city, and loved seeing the Folsom Street sign. It seemed to Zachary that he'd been gone for years and was pleasantly amazed to see that things had remained the same.

Zachary was tired, but he didn't want to go to bed. He wanted to walk around his rooms, soak up the familiar sights and smells. He called Leslie while Sali took a bath and thanked him. Could the two of them "talk tomorrow?" Zachary pleaded, using nerves and exhaustion as the excuse for the apparent lack of gratitude.

"Of course, my boy. That you're home and safe makes me as happy as a shoe salesman with a foot fetish. But tomorrow you'll have to bring me up to date on this ghastly adventure and introduce me to the child bride."

It was late in the East. It was very late for Jeremiah Tower to suddenly summon the pilots. The phone call he'd received, however, was both absurd and disturbing and he could no longer trust any of his people for direct intervention.

As Tower understood it, Bernard Manning had killed his captor and escaped. No one knew where he was or what he knew or didn't know; or what he had or didn't have. That was the disturbing part. The absurd part was that some strange fairy and his little Mexican sidekick had killed at least two operatives, at least one of them Tower's. Could there be a third party in on this?

Even though he could still control the damage, he could not afford even such minor disasters—after all, it was a petty burglary that brought down Nixon, allowing first an idiot and then a southern populist to fuck up the timetable for the new world order.

As the Hawker Siddley 125 lifted off, Tower folded the book flap, marking his place in *Bonfire* and went to the teak cabinet for a bottle of port. This part of the plane looked like a small cocktail lounge in an elegant hotel. Depending on whether his private craft had a tail or head wind, the trip should take five or six hours. He took the bottle, a glass, and the book with him to the bedroom.

No use trying to determine what to do about all this until he got there and understood the situation. One of his rules was never to speculate.

21 "You want something to eat?" Zachary asked Sali, who came out of the bathroom, wrapped in a towel.

"I never see . . . ," he said, then stopped and corrected himself. ". . . have seen a towel this big in somebody's bathroom. The beach maybe, but not so smooth like this." Sali's light cocoa-colored body was covered from head to foot in the ivory bath towel.

"How about some waffles? I really don't have much else until we do some shopping."

"That's okay." Sali looked around. "This is like a mansion, Zachary."

"A very small mansion," Zachary said, pleased that Sali was calling him by name, pleased too, that the youth was too overwhelmed to engage in his usually flirtatious behavior.

"You have so much," Sali said, following Zachary into the kitchen. "All for you? Nobody else?"

"No," Zachary said. Sali's black hair was wet and shone like a raven's. He looked so innocent, chaste even—the deep brown eyes lost for the moment, the turn of the neck, the long, delicate fingers clutching the towel closed. Sali seemed neither male nor female, an almost spiritual form.

"You own so many beautiful things," Sali said. "Does it bother you that someone might come and take something beautiful away?"

"Only recently," Zachary said.

Manny, stepping out into the grayish, dawn light, looked like a tourist, a tourist of the worst variety. The fellow who'd determined Manny's fashion statement either had a perverse sense of humor or a bad case of gringo stereotyping, or both. Just as well. Perhaps he would go unnoticed as he had breakfast and tried to plan his exit.

On his way to the restaurant he looked at the still desolate streets. This time of day, a stakeout would be obvious. He figured there was at least one man left—the one that helped Earl Patrick drag Manny from the sea, undressed him, and tossed him into the hole. Manny felt no special animosity toward him—just wanted to avoid future contact.

No restaurants were open. Manny walked down by the docks. The Caprice was gone. Manny went back to his room. In a few hours he'd grab a ride to another hotel and make flight arrangements.

He felt surprisingly good. He wouldn't want to engage anyone in a wrestling match, not even a beautiful *señorita,* but he felt good enough to get out of there, good enough to get on with his life in a way that wasn't so hazardous to his health. And thinking about health, he suddenly realized he hadn't had a drink in quite a while.

He went over to the window and looked out over the street below, watching the sun rise over the ocean, watching the people begin to scamper on the palm-tree lined street. It could've been a nice trip. He and Zachary could have enjoyed themselves.

The last time he saw Zachary was at the beach. He had been rude to Zachary who, try as Manny did, couldn't be pried from some sort of innate passivity, not even from the passivity of his beach chair for a dip in the ocean.

And that's when Manny was plucked from the sea. Shit, it was Zachary who knew where Manny would be and when. In fact, only Zachary could have known when he went to see the woman, unless someone was watching him closely. Zachary could have easily placed a call and someone could have easily gotten to the woman before he did. It was clear in Manny's mind now. He remembered repeating the address on the phone in Zachary's presence, believing, perhaps stupidly, that Zachary could not speak Spanish.

Certainly, there was some reason he'd been assigned to Zachary Grayson. A setup? Someone to watch him. Someone to watch the courier. Perhaps the docile food writer made the contact himself, picked up whatever it was that his employer needed and allowed Manny to be dumped into the hands of the enemy as a diversion.

Manny picked up the phone, got the operator, and in a few moments heard the phone ringing. Manny felt relief rather than anger hearing Zachary's voice. In a strange way, Zachary was the closest thing to a friend Manny had ever had. Guilty or innocent, he was glad the guy made it back alive. He hung up immediately, went downstairs and checked out of his room.

"Who was it so early?" Sali asked as Zachary put the phone back in the cradle.

"Go back to sleep," Zachary said. "No one. Wrong number."

Sali snuggled closer. "What do we do today?"

"Whatever we want. I thought maybe we would go to Macy's or Nordstrom, get you some jeans and sweatshirts, shoes, normal things."

"Normal things?" Sali asked, grinning.

"Yes, normal things. You can't go running around half-naked in San Francisco."

"Why can't I?"

"Too cold."

Sali laughed. "But this is California."

"No it isn't, it's San Francisco."

Though the sun was up in its own faint way, Zachary had already missed his morning ritual. Furthermore, he was pretty sure he wouldn't be able to get back to normal things himself for a few days until he got Sali accustomed to the city. He climbed out of bed, slipped on his robe and went to the bathroom to run cold water over his face.

"Are you up for good?" Zachary shouted out. But he got no answer. He toweled his face, looked in the mirror. He had some color to show for the trip, though hardly the tan he'd expected.

He came back into the bedroom, but Sali was gone. Zachary headed through the short hall into the living room. "Sali?"

"I've got him, I'm afraid," Leslie said, standing in the doorway with a large paper bag. Sali, who'd thrown on one of Zachary's undershirts, looked back at Zachary. "We're just getting to know one another," Leslie continued.

"A friend of yours?" Sali said with not so subtle disdain.

"He's positively delightful . . . in his way." Leslie grinned. "I was sure you'd be up by now and I was also sure you wouldn't have your usual provisions, so I took it upon my charitable self to pick up some goodies at the bakery and some extraordinary jam."

"Come in," Zachary said. "Sali, this is the gentleman who sent the plane for us," then turning to Leslie, "for which I shall be eternally grateful."

"I'm afraid you will be billed," Leslie said, coming into the room and heading for the kitchen. "I have no idea how much, but you might have to mortgage your condo."

"Gladly," Zachary said as he and Sali followed.

"That was your airplane?" Sali asked.

"Oh no, my dear, a friend of a friend. We were quite lucky the owner was on his yacht."

"As I said, I am eternally grateful."

"Yes, yes, of course. If you'll just fix some of your wonderful Vienna-style coffee and tell me about your extraordinary adventure, detailing, of course, the saga of your green-eyed playmate, your eternal debt shall be made finite."

Sali looked at Zachary, who caught the look of anxiety in his eyes.

"Manny wasn't a playmate, Leslie. He was a house guest," Zachary said, aware of Leslie's natural trouble-making instincts.

"Yes, yes, so be it." Leslie grinned. "Get on with it."

"Manny went swimming in the ocean and didn't come back." Zachary put some shiny brown beans in the grinder. "A woman he had talked to was murdered. There was an attempt on my life, which Sali foiled. We were subsequently followed somehow and another unsuccessful attempt was made on our lives. If it weren't for Sali, I'd be dead. Twice."

"Goodness gracious. To think my Zachary here was all caught up in some sort of James Bond thing. It has to be connected to Manny, doesn't it? No one could possibly be after you for anything. I've never met such a harmless creature."

"I don't know," Zachary said. "It's all a mystery."

"You must have some clue," Leslie continued.

"We . . . ," Zachary began to answer.

"Who knows?" Sali interjected quickly, glancing at Zachary. ". . . have no idea."

"This is so exciting, my dear. It's extraordinary, this spy novel thing. Perhaps there's a magnificent diamond involved, you know, like the Pink Panther. International diamond smugglers. Drugs more likely. You must begin at the beginning, tell me every juicy detail."

"There's not a whole lot to say," Zachary said. The *whirr* of the grinder kept everybody quiet for a few moments. By the time it stopped, Leslie had seated himself next to Sali, leaning into the boy conspiratorially.

"Now, my charming child, let's begin with how you two met," Leslie said. "Somehow, I suspect it wasn't at a dinner party."

"Well you see, Leslie," Sali said, glancing up at Zachary with a grin spreading across his face, "I just got back from Barcelona where I met with my friend Juan Carlos, you know, the King of Spain. . . ."

Jeremiah Tower had checked into the Huntington Hotel on Nob Hill mid-morning. The trip had been restful and in fact, after his glass of port and finishing the *Bonfires* book, he slept comfortably for three hours.

He'd already made two important phone calls, one to a local contact getting assurance that things were once again under control and advising him to wait. The Arab had been unduly concerned. The worm had indeed turned. All it took was the right combination of incentives—death and money. The subject was, as it turned out, a pragmatist. The other call was to room service. Jeremiah had finished breakfast and sat in one of the comfortable chairs with a third cup of decaf coffee, a copy of *USA Today*, the *San Francisco Chronicle*, and the *New York Times*.

Despite the abundance of reading material, he was disappointed that he was unable to get the *Washington Post*. His morning was incomplete without the wonderfully readable, but highly disagreeable *Post*. He thought about contacting some of his more important clients in San Francisco. It was debatable. He wasn't sure he wanted to document his presence here. Though he was not one to doubt himself or his decisions, he was not sure it was wise to make the trip after all. He'd been roused out of his sleep by the call. Perhaps, without benefit of a crystal-clear mind, he'd been too hasty.

Manny decided to go for broke—that is, he'd cause Earl Patrick's employer an expensive outlay of cash. When he got to the elegant resort hotel just outside the main village, Manny reserved an additional room under the name of Enzio Palmeri. At three separate travel agencies he charged three airline tickets, each for a different member of his fictional family to three different destinations, on Patrick's American Express. One of them was for Enzio Palmeri to Los Angeles.

Next, he went to the expensive shops at several of the hotels and bought clothes more suitable than the *turista* outfit he'd been stuck with, and managed to find a nice pair of Ralph Lauren glasses. When he went back to his room, he gelled his hair, applied a little color to his burgeoning mustache, and when he was done he looked like a young European traveler.

Dressed up as the new "him," Manny went back downstairs and registered in the second room as Enzio Palmeri.

He marveled a bit at the evolution of Bernard Manning, who arrived cocky and in jeans, then spent a few days absolutely naked in a tanker, trudged into town looking like a monster from a bad horror flick, then a tourist in a bad horror flick, and now a wealthy and probably spoiled Italian playboy.

Next he took a taxi from the hotel to the airport. He exchanged his pesos for dollars. He now had five thousand in greenbacks. He would board a plane to Los Angeles. Then freedom. A little scary. There was absolutely no one he could trust. Not even his own employer. And frankly, he didn't have a life—with or without his employer.

Bernard Manning was aware that he was a small fish and he knew that he knew little, if anything, of importance to anyone—either about this strange organization he worked for or about the enemies of that organization. Perhaps they—both of them, all of them—would merely let him go. Perhaps not. He thought again about being born in the Year of the Rabbit. It seemed even more fitting. He would be running now, his rabbit nose twitching at the remotest of possible dangers. He'd be running now, without knowing if anyone was in pursuit.

He didn't dare go back to Key West to retrieve his meager belongings and his equally meager savings, nor could he even retrieve any of his former identities. Manny cursed himself for not being more farsighted. He should have put a cache of dough away somewhere and had an available identity in the event this happened. But he'd lived as the grasshopper, not the ant. He drank and caroused his way through life, from dismal paycheck to dismal paycheck.

At this point, it was too dangerous to use his current sources in the creation of some new identity.

Even "Enzio" would have to be discarded in Los Angeles because it was possible they could track him that far if, in fact, he could make it that far. If he made it, he would have only a five-thousand dollar stake and a suitcase full of decent clothes to begin again. Manny would have to become an entirely new person, in an entirely new place.

By noon, Leslie appeared to be exhausted by the questions he'd asked, for which there were few answers. Zachary assured him that his speculations were far more interesting than anything they knew and that their experience was more nightmare than adventure.

Leslie departed, suggesting that Zachary might now have something worthy of memoirs. "Very few chefs," he said, "have endured assassination attempts."

It was obvious to Zachary and, Zachary believed, equally obvious to Leslie, that Sali didn't like his new neighbor; Zachary expected Sali to go on about him after he left. He did not. By one-thirty, he and Sali were on their way to Macy's. This evening, Zachary would take his new roommate to the Elite Café for dinner.

If the timing was right, Zachary would try to find out what was on Sali's mind about the future. If nothing else, the fine food and the familiar surroundings would help calm Zachary's mind, which had not been convinced the ordeal was over.

Jeremiah Tower met with his contact over dinner at the Clift House and decided he could return to Washington—that to do this thing correctly would take a little time. No longer fearing that his presence in San Francisco was a problem, he took a few more days to visit the chairman of a large, international corporation, from whose patronage Tower's foundation benefited and over which much of what was done by it was influenced. The Iraqi situation had made their relationship even more important. He could assuage their concerns in this matter. All in all, the decision to fly out was wise after all, and it was now a legitimate expense that didn't have to be manipulated for the I.R.S., the only government agency that presented him any real danger.

Dinner did help Zachary. Sali, in his new clothes, was not only in good humor but was devouring the attention of the waiters, both of whom overlooked the fact that Zachary had slipped him half a glass of wine. Sali was full of ideas and reacted with enthusiasm to the idea that he might attend one of the local universities.

The days and nights that followed were easy. Sali spent a good deal of his time with and without Zachary, wandering the city, getting accustomed to mass transit, the neighborhoods, and especially the schools. He picked up all the literature he could find on each and read them in the evening while Zachary's increasingly calm mind fixed on some book or other.

Zachary was able to slip out of bed early, while Sali slept, and get back into his routine. Sali stayed up late and watched endless movies on the cable Zachary had installed for that purpose. Sali eventually dropped his defenses with regard to Leslie, who refused to give up winning him over.

The coup came the night Leslie invited Zachary and Sali to the opera. Though it was no surprise to Leslie, the fact that Sali completely enjoyed it, raved about it, was a surprise to Zachary, who felt a mild wave of jealousy as his two friends babbled endlessly, it seemed, about what they had seen and liked.

They soon became a threesome. Usually in the afternoons,

after Leslie disposed of his mysterious business dealings and Zachary worked on his new book, they would pick some sort of cultural object to attack. Museums, galleries, the Palace of Fine Arts. Sometimes it was a neighborhood. They spent an entire day on Union Street, walking the length of it on one side of the street, then coming back on the other side, bobbing in and out of shops.

They took the ferry to Sausalito, rented a car for a day's excursion to San Gregorio beach. They planned weekend trips, too—the curious little town of Mendocino, up the coast; as well as Napa and Sonoma and the surrounding wine country. They had plans for longer trips—to Russian River and as far away as Lake Tahoe and Palm Springs.

Sali was happy. No place was uninteresting. He was never bored—not even with Leslie's excrutiatingly long diatribes which now focused on educating the youth. Leslie, pleased to have an appreciative audience and a resident gourmet to suggest the best from the menus of the best restaurants, was full of energy. In fact, it was Zachary who tired first, and if anyone, it was Zachary who slipped out of the festive mood from time to time.

Sali seemed to sense Zachary's occasional bouts with insecurity. At those times, he'd grab Zachary's arm. "You are the most important person in my life," he'd say. Or, "You know how happy you make me?" Once he announced at a little restaurant in North Beach, where the three of them dined on Italian sausage and where Leslie became a little too proprietory, that Zachary was his father and his lover.

For a second, Leslie looked like the wind had been knocked out of him. Then he made a sly remark subtly suggesting the boy knew which side of the slice his bread was buttered on, recouped, and managed to talk them all into roars of laughter which made them forget the discourteous remark.

But if the truth were known, Zachary was the happiest at night, when it was just the two of them. He now even looked forward to being dragged from sleep by Sali, fresh from his nightly shower, climbing into bed and either snuggling quietly next to him to sleep, or on occasion, not so quietly snuggling with no intention of either of them sleeping.

Zachary had also begun to think that all of this playtime was not in Sali's best interest—that going to a university might offer him a little more at this stage than a whirlwind of party-time activity. Surprisingly, Sali agreed and soon he was back at the college pamphlets and schedules. Zachary, who knew very few people well, did in fact know many important people well enough. He was sure they could maneuver Sali past the bureaucracies that put impenetrable veils around such things as citizenship, high-school degrees, and the like.

22 Leslie took it less kindly each time Zachary postponed some previously discussed trip and bowed out on Leslie's suggestion for the afternoon excursions.

When Zachary returned home from a long-promised interview with Frances Moffat, columnist for the *Nob Hill Gazette*, at the Opera Café on Van Ness, he found Sali missing. Occasionally, Sali would go across the hall and talk with Leslie. That would explain the absence of the usual note.

"Is Sali here?" Zachary said, nudging open the door to Leslie's condo and finding Leslie seated on his rather uncomfortable Zen couch.

"Gone," came Leslie's turgid reply.

"Gone?"

"Yes. And whether he returns depends entirely on you."

Zachary felt like he'd been hit in the stomach. There wasn't a siblant "s" in Leslie's speech and his face was hard. This was not one of Leslie's amusing games. Zachary retraced the morning's events to see if something had been said that would make Sali want to leave. There had been no arguments, no hint that Sali was unhappy.

In fact, they had laughed just this morning and talked about San Francisco State University over breakfast and had even planned on taking in a movie after dinner.

"I don't understand," Zachary said. For a horrible and fleeting moment he thought maybe Sali had found someone his own age during his independent meanderings around town. But there'd been no clue, no change in Sali's closeness or affection.

"Oh, I think you do. It's about a little trip to Mexico."

"Sali went back to Mexico?" Zachary said in disbelief.

"Of course not, Zachary. You've simply waded into water very much over your head. There are some people who believe you have something that belongs to them."

Suddenly everything made sense. He knew what this was all about. Zachary went to the window. He didn't want to look at Leslie. He looked down in what he knew was a futile hope of seeing Sali bouncing up the hill.

"What have you done with him?"

"Well, at least we don't have to go through hours of denial. You somehow got yourself involved in this."

"When I called you for help, I gave you our location, didn't I?"

"Oh yes, then you thought the lines might be tapped. I had to get you back here. The computer chip. That's all we wanted."

"And anybody who got in the way was expendable?"

"It's called 'collateral damage,' Zachary. We don't intend or want it to happen. It's merely an unfortunate circumstance of the operation that is, not too incidentally, much larger than us in scope. The greater good, I'm afraid."

"For whom?"

"You are not that important in the scheme of things. Nor am I. It isn't personal."

"That makes me feel a whole lot better."

"I tried everything, Zachary, to get what I wanted and keep you out of it. I meant to use you without you knowing. Blame your handsome sidekick, Bernard Manning. He got you into this."

"And Manny?"

Leslie laughed. "Well, you see, that was a prize piece of deception. Manny was working for the . . . the opposition, let's say. I had someone in the pipeline. There's a despicable Cuban in Miami—I understand he makes me look like an elf—who works both sides. I had Manny's instructions altered so that he would be near me so that I would know when and exactly where the pickup was to be made. I had no idea he'd be so good-looking. I was amused and thought it was a nice thing for you. I did not plan your going with him and if you remember, even tried to talk you out of it. That's why I had the dinner party. Then another surprise. I certainly didn't plan for you to hook up with the delivery boy as well. What's the line: 'Fools go where angels fear to tread'?"

"What are you going to do with Sali?"

"As I said, that depends on you and him. I'm terribly sorry. I really am. It's so sad. You lived such a safe life, comfortable, harmless. You preyed on no one, hurt no one. I tried to tell you as best I could." Leslie shook his head, the extra flesh on his neck quivering. He pursed his lips. "It's that way in war, you know. The generals usually live. So do the dictators and presidents and kings. It is always the gullible youth led to slaughter, the naive philosophers who are disillusioned, jailed, or killed when they finally discover the real brutality of the world. It's the women and children who die from the bombs and the gas and the cannons. But, Zachary, that's the way it is."

"Spare me your thoughts on the meaning of life. What is this all about? What is it that everybody wants that is so valuable?"

"It's a little computer chip," he said, grinning. "I'd hoped you'd know that. And I'd hoped you'd know where it was."

"And what makes this little computer chip so valuable?"

"I have no idea."

"No idea. You're willing to kidnap and kill and you don't know what it is? Who is it for, Leslie?"

"Well, let me put it this way, you won't be a traitor if you give it to me or have Sali give it to me."

"Not that it matters, but will I be a traitor if I don't?"

Leslie laughed again, this time heartily. "Ooooh, not really, Zachary. It really doesn't concern you or Sali. It would have had no impact on your lives or mine, for that matter."

"So tell me about Sali."

"Let's talk about what you know first."

"I know nothing."

"You've already admitted you know something. One of you has to have the answers. Sali is with Fassir and your boy will be a long time dying, if you know what I mean. Incidentally, when you said, 'Will I be a traitor if I don't,' the operative word was 'don't' not 'can't'. You'd be a terrible spy."

Zachary turned back from the window, looking at this unlikely villain. He tried desperately to control both his anger and the turmoil of his internal organs.

"I'm not a spy. I have nothing to hide. I don't know what or where it is or who wants it or why." Zachary moved toward Leslie but stopped when he saw the chrome-plated pistol emerge from Leslie's jacket.

"Even if you don't, Sali probably does. We do not believe that your friend Manny ever got his hands on it. That means that Sali either has it, or knows where it is. He was the last to have it."

"A gun, Leslie?"

"Yes, it's making me a nervous wreck, but this is serious business, Zachary. Very serious business. I can't seem to get through to you. At this very moment, your little Latino friend is on his way to Chinatown. I sent him on a little errand. Also, at this very moment, Fassir is on his way to Chinatown. Fassir has a way of getting what he wants."

Leslie paused, waiting for Zachary's response. When none came, Leslie continued.

"Sali is a beautiful young man. Fassir has some peculiar fetishes. He will enjoy his work. Where are you going?"

Zachary was halfway to the door. "Out!"

"No you're not." Leslie raised the pistol and though his hand shook, there was no question about the look on his face or the tone in his voice. "Don't let my being an old queen lead you to some incredibly false assumptions. I *will* kill you. Not happily. Besides, you'd be of no help to Sali dead."

"All right, Leslie. You win. I don't know where it is; but I'm willing to tell you everything I know. Perhaps we can piece it together."

"That's quite a relief, Zachary, my boy. Why don't you sit down over there and we'll have a little chat."

"My mind is a little fuzzy. I had quite a bit of wine at lunch. Is it all right to make some coffee first?"

"Delightful idea. Why don't you make it?" Leslie followed Zachary to the kitchen. "The coffee's up there."

As Zachary measured and filled the little white filter and measured and poured the water into the kettle, he explained how Manny had some phone conversations and private meetings with someone Zachary presumed was the murdered woman.

"So exactly, and I mean exactly, how did you meet your charming urchin?"

"One more thing I have to do. I have to go to the bathroom. The wine."

"Sure. This little mystery has been simmering over a month now. A few more minutes means little to me, though I am expecting a call from Fassir and that has a lot to do with the boy."

"I understand."

There was no window, or phone, or any weapon capable of competing with a pistol in the bathroom and Leslie was content to wait behind the closed door.

"Thank God," Zachary thought, "I really have to go."

When Zachary came out, he explained how he'd gone to the beach and was waiting for Manny when Sali approached him with an offer to read his palm.

"A fortune teller as well, my goodness." Leslie laughed.

Zachary poured the hot water into the filter and coffee spilled into the clear glass container below. "Yes, he said I would live a long, long time. You take artificial sweetener, don't you?"

"I don't know why, surely a few more pounds in my present state wouldn't make much difference." Leslie reached into a little container and tossed Zachary two little packets of Nutrasweet. "Two actually."

"Do you have cream?" Zachary asked.

"You don't take cream."

"My stomach is a little uneasy right now."

"Of course," Leslie said.

As Leslie opened the refrigerator, Zachary slid the little white packet he'd extracted from his wallet while he was in the bathroom between the two packets of Nutrasweet, tearing all three simultaneously. The contents went into the cup on the right. He poured the cream into the cup on the left, then poured the coffee under Leslie's careful gaze.

"Go on," Leslie said.

"Well, Sali stole my watch while he was reading my palm."

"Clever little bugger."

Seated back in the living room, Zachary told Leslie about Sali breaking into Zachary's room because he felt guilty and wanted to return the watch without having to face his victim and, instead, foiled the murder attempt on Zachary.

"He brought your watch back to you, is that right? My goodness." Leslie smiled.

"Yes. You haven't touched your coffee, Leslie."

"You can't get the flavor when it's too hot. In a moment. Meanwhile, I'd like you to take off your watch. There's a little penknife in the desk drawer. I want you to open the back of it."

"My God, you're right," Zachary said, more than willing to trade a stupid computer chip for Sali's life.

Zachary went to the desk, found the knife, and quickly pried the back from the watch. The little chip fell to the floor. Zachary picked it up and put it on the table beside Leslie. He thought Leslie would be happy, but he wasn't smiling.

"You have it, the mystery is solved."

"Yes," Leslie said, picking up his cup of coffee.

"Leslie. . . ." Zachary intended to warn him, but Leslie interrupted.

"Unfortunately, it doesn't really change anything."

"What?"

"Zachary, we are all fools. But there are fools and lesser fools. You, sweet as you are, are of the grander variety. All of this represents a tragedy—the fall of charm, wit, even intelligence, in a fashion. These are rare finds in this world and I deeply regret making them rarer."

"So, you are going to kill us, both of us. No matter."

"Zachary, Zachary, Zachary, for such a bright, literate fellow, you are so incredibly naive. I tried, Zachary. I tried. I convinced my superior to take the time so that I could have this kind of conversation with you without you knowing. If only you'd told me this little story when I asked a long time ago."

"I'm sorry, too," Zachary said, as Leslie took an unhealthy sip of cooled coffee.

Calmly, Zachary took Leslie's cup to the kitchen and poured its contents down the drain. He let the tap water run until it steamed against the cool aluminum of the sink. He rinsed the cup again and again and let the hot water run, almost dumbly staring at the flow. Suddenly, to break the strange, almost hypnotic gaze, he jerked the faucet off. Then he walked back into the living room, sitting at the desk. He stared at the telephone and waited.

Zachary had no idea how much time had passed. The sunlight that illumined the Koji-style windows earlier now had no luminosity whatsoever and Leslie's stark, modern living room, full of straight lines and harsh angles, was as dull and as lifeless as the corpse sitting grotesquely on the sofa. Finally, the strange electronic ring jolted him from his numbness.

"Hello?" Zachary said.

"Who's this?" the voice said.

"This is Zachary. Fassir?"

There was a long pause, then a tentative, "Yes."

"It's all right. Leslie said for you to bring the boy here."

"May I talk with Leslie?"

"I'm afraid you can't. He went over to my place. He got a call. Long distance, I think. He knew you were going to call so he asked me to wait here and talk to you while he called this person back on my phone." There was a long pause. Zachary was afraid. He didn't want to lose him. "He said to tell you that . . . he's sure he can get it. But he needs Sali. I'm a little puzzled by it. I mean it's mysterious and all, but he said to tell you it was important the boy come back here."

"I tell you what, I'll call back in a few minutes," Fassir said.

"Oh, well, okay . . . , " Zachary stalled. "But he did say he had a lot of calls to make." It was almost as if someone else were talking, someone calm, in charge, confident. It was the same calm he had when he saw Sali in the hands of those men on the street corner in Puerto Vallarta. "But, of course, I'll tell him whatever you want. I'm just a confused messenger, that's all." Had he said too much? Could Fassir detect the tension, the nervousness in his voice? Zachary didn't think so. This bizarre clearheadedness was still there. It seemed to come from some reservoir in his brain that Zachary wasn't familiar with. "What shall I tell Leslie?"

"Tell him I'm on my way," Fassir said.

It took a few moments before Zachary realized he was now listening to the dial tone.

* * *

There would be another wait, this time for Fassir. Zachary lifted Leslie's hefty body to a chair so that Fassir would see only the back of his head and part of his arm. Zachary moved the phone over to the chair so that the cord across the rug would be obvious. He took the receiver out of the cradle and stuck it between Leslie's neck and shoulder.

Zachary, his sweaty palm curled around the handle of Leslie's pistol, sat on the sofa precisely where Leslie had been seated, the hand with the gun burrowed behind the seat cushions.

There were questions now. What would he do with Fassir? Give him the chip? So what? He'd already done that with Leslie and it made no difference. No doubt the possession of the gun, the pad of his finger already pressed against the metal trigger, implied he'd already answered that question. But should he, could he do it? If Fassir lived, he would live only to kill another day.

There are the proper authorities. There is a system of justice. There were police, weren't there? Police, judges, and jury? The killing of Leslie was done to save Sali. How could Zachary assume the role of executioner if Sali were returned?

And so the police might arrest Fassir. And so he might be convicted. Might. There would be others. There were others in Mexico. Yes, there would be others, anyway. Others who would not want him or Sali to testify.

23 "Zachary . . . , " Fassir said, standing in the doorway with Sali silent and in front of him.

"Fassir, nice to see you again." Sali looked puzzled. "Thank you for bringing the boy." Sali's eyes filled with tears, but his mouth curled in contempt. He had been betrayed. "I'm sure Leslie will be off the phone in a minute. He's apparently enduring someone else's monologue for a change. Come over and sit by me Sali, we've found the chip, everything's all right."

Sali glared at Zachary, looked up at Fassir, who nodded. Instead of moving toward the sofa, Sali walked away and to the far end of the room. Just as well, Zachary thought. Fassir's drawn pistol was apparent now, and it seemed like an eternity before he tucked it back inside his jacket.

"That's good news," Fassir said, but he appeared unsure. His mind overruled his instinct.

Sali turned, his eyes falling on Leslie's contorted face. He looked back at Zachary, eyes wide in disbelief.

"I told you everything would be fine, Sali."

Fassir's hand went toward his jacket. Zachary's hand rose, arm extended. Zachary could see the flash of metal come out from Fassir's coat. Zachary's hand was steady, his vision was clear. He fired. Fassir swatted his head as if it had been a fly. His revolver was out.

Calm still, Zachary fired again. There was only a small hole in Fassir's forehead; but behind him blood splattered against the door. Fassir remained standing for what seemed a very long time. Then his legs simply buckled at the knees. He seemed to fall into himself, crumpling to the floor like a laundry bag.

Sali brought Zachary's arm down and removed the gun from the clenched fist. He wiped it off with his shirt, pressed it into Leslie's hand for a second, then layed it on the table. He picked up the computer chip.

"Leave it," Zachary said, finally standing up, his knees weak. "It doesn't matter."

Sali put it back where he found it.

While Sali showered, Zachary called the police. He told the 911 operator he heard shots next door and was afraid to find out what was going on. When the police arrived, Zachary explained that other than hearing what sounded like a shot, he knew nothing else.

"We can't be sure, but it looks like the old guy shot the other guy then died of a heart attack or something."

"I'm really sorry," Zachary said.

"Judging by what we found in there, it was probably a lovers' quarrel or something like that. Did you know your neighbor very well?"

"Actually, not at all well," Zachary said. "I'm not very sociable."

The policeman thanked him and left.

"You are sociable with me. I hope." Sali came into the room wrapped in a towel.

"I'm learning to be."

"Looks like we're gonna have to stick together now, Zach."

"Why is that?" Zach said, failing to hold back the smile.

"To protect each other."

"Hello," Manny said, his voice an octave or two deeper, rising from the torpor of sleep. "Just a minute." He inched his way closer to the sleeping body next to him and nudged the delicate shoulder. "Jenny?"

"Hmmmn." She rolled over into him, kissed his neck.

"Phone." He crawled over the side of the bed and stumbled toward the bathroom. It was funny, he still couldn't navigate in the morning; and all these years he thought it was because of his drinking. Apparently alcohol had nothing to do with it. He just wasn't a fucking morning person.

He could still hear Jenny's voice, though the words were muffled by the distance.

A hint of last night's dream crept into his brain, but he couldn't catch it—a furry night creature frightened by the day.

For a moment he thought about Zachary and his recurring nightmares. Wondered if he still had them. He had thought about writing, but then he couldn't be sure, could he? For Manny, Zachary remained a mystery. Good friend? Devious foe? Whatever he really was, he was, in Manny's mind, forever sitting in his beach chair looking out at the sea.

Jenny was off the phone, her short blond hair pressed

against a stack of pillows. "When do you have to go, Phillipe?" she asked as he crawled in beside her.

"I don't know. Maybe never."

"That would be nice." Her finger traced his lips. He pulled the sheet up over their heads, the two of them encased in a little cocoon. "What do you see when you close your eyes?" she asked.

He shut his eyes. "A big . . . vast, empty universe."

"Room for me out there?"

Manny didn't know how he felt about that.

"I don't know."

"You two know each other, don't you?" asked the ex–Vice President as he and Senator Hedges nudged in next to Jeremiah Tower at the hotel bar.

"Mortal friends," Tower said, his steel gray eyes pouncing on Senator Hedges.

Hedges kept his smile as the former heartbeat-away was plucked from the bar and led by his wife to another gathering of suits.

"No hard feelings," Hedges said to Tower when they were alone.

Tower raised one bushy eyebrow. "No hard feelings."

They looked at each other curiously for a moment, not sure they had understood each other exactly right. Tower picked up his drink from the bar and moved away, shaking his head. Of course Hedges had the chip. If he didn't, who did?

The woman hired to clean Leslie's condo heard something metallic being sucked up the hose of the vacuum—a dime by the sound of it, she thought. Not enough to take the damn machine apart.

198

EPILOGUE

Dear Diary,

I know I said I wouldn't write you anymore. I changed my mind. I've changed my mind quite a bit lately. I've changed my mind about jazz, for example. With Sali's tutoring, I've learned a lot of new things.

A wonderful lady, whom I met before this awful affair began, has moved across the hall—where Leslie used to live. Her name is Alva Burdine, a gallery owner and painter. She's taken a liking to Sali—us, really. Sali adores her. Henry, her assistant, who was so warm and friendly at our first meeting, has suddenly become aloof. Nevertheless, Alva has invited us to an opening tonight. Though it is quite unlike me, we're going.

Strangely, I do miss Leslie. However, while I feel an incredible sadness when I think of him, I have come to terms with what I did. I also wonder about Manny from time to time. I'll always remember the night he brought me a glass of milk after one of my nightmares. It was something he seemed to understand all too clearly.

Perhaps I should have called, let someone know he is missing. But who would I call? What would I say? Missing from whom; where? Fortunately, the nightmares seem to have disappeared. So has the foxglove. The light, where those old-fashioned flowers grew, was just right for those silvery-green Japanese ferns Sali loves so much.

Zachary, San Francisco